Ahmed Taibaoui is a professor at the Fness, and Management Sciences at the Ur ria. He was awarded the Tayeb Salih Inter Creativity (2014) for his novel *Mawt na'im* (Death of a Sleeper), as well as the President of the Republic Award for Young Innovators (2011) for his novel *al-Maqam al-'ali* (The High Eminence). He lives in Algiers.

Jonathan Wright is a translator and former Reuters journalist. His previous translations from the Arabic include Khaled Al Khamissi's *Taxi*, Youssef Ziedan's *Azazeel* (winner of the International Prize for Arabic Fiction, 2009), Saud Alsanousi's *The Bamboo Stalk* (winner of the IPAF, 2013), Hammour Ziada's *The Longing of the Dervish* (winner of the Naguib Mahfouz Prize), Ahmed Saadawi's *Frankenstein in Baghdad* (shortlisted for the Man Booker International Prize), Mazen Maarouf's *Jokes for the Gunmen* (shortlisted for the Man Booker International Prize), and Hassan Blasim's *God 99, The Madman of Freedom Square,* and *The Iraqi Christ* (winner of the 2014 Independent Foreign Fiction Prize). He lives in London.

The Disappearance of Mr. Nobody

A novel by Ahmed Taibaoui

Translated from the Arabic by
Jonathan Wright

hoopoe

AN IMPRINT OF AUC PRESS

First published in 2023 by Hoopoe
113 Sharia Kasr el Aini, Cairo, Egypt
One Rockefeller Plaza, 10th Floor, New York, NY 10020
www.hoopoefiction.com

Hoopoe is an imprint of The American University in Cairo Press
www.aucpress.com

ISBN 978 1 649 03214 0

Library of Congress Cataloging-in-Publication Data

Names: Ṭībāwī, Aḥmad, author. | Wright, Jonathan, 1953- translator.
Title: The disappearance of Mr Nobody / Ahmed Taibaoui ; translated by
  Jonathan Wright.
Identifiers: LCCN 2022017788 | ISBN 9781649032157 (hardback) | ISBN
  9781649032140 (trade paperback) | ISBN 9781649032164 (epub) | ISBN
  9781649032171 (adobe pdf)
Subjects: LCGFT: Noir fiction. | Novels.
Classification: LCC PJ7964.I23 I4413 2022 | DDC 892.7/37--dc23/
eng/20220429

1 2 3 4 5   27 26 25 24 23

Designed by Adam el-Sehemy

The Man Who Took His Face Off and Left

1

Evasion

I HAVE A KNIFE IN my kitchen. I've never been an aggressive person, but if this disgusting old man goes on jabbering away I'm seriously thinking of finding a new use for that knife. I'll cut his tongue out, and some other organ if necessary. I'm out of cigarettes, the weather's so miserable it makes you aggressive and, on top of all that, he's giving me good reason to finish him off. Removing someone from the land of the living might be a reasonable solution, even for someone like me who has only trivial reasons for doing so. This Uncle Mubarak, as everyone calls him, is an uncle to everyone, not an uncle to anyone in particular. He's public property, vulgar and delusional. He likes to hear people say things that suggest he's respected, though he doesn't deserve any respect. That's what I learned in his café when I had the impression he deserved a certain respect in deference to his gray hair. It was my mistake from the beginning—when I opened the door and let him into this den of mine, and earlier when I let him break down the barrier I had set up between myself and others. Being alone is bad, but having to deal with other people is worse. I haven't spoken to anyone for days. I've sold my phone. I don't have anyone to call or anyone to call me. Throughout the past year, Mubarak is the only person I've spoken to for more than five minutes.

He's still nattering away. I turn on the television, which has served no purpose since I came to live here. He's trying to prove to me that somehow he understands everything that's happening in the world. The Jews are the cause of all the misfortunes and intrigues that have befallen us, he told me. This is his second visit to me. It's close to nine o'clock in the evening. I have a little balcony that looks out on a square that's surrounded by buildings and frequented at night by lecherous dogs and cats. I often sit there and stay up till dawn. Silence is wisdom, he says in summation.

I'll spit in his face or take my clothes off and sit down naked with him so that he goes off and leaves me. My suspicions tell me that that's what he wants. He deprives me of my only outlet—sitting on the balcony and observing the banality of the world when it's shrouded in darkness, or reading by a low light that doesn't draw the attention of my neighbors. I do that after midnight and sometimes I even worry that the glow at the end of my cigarette might give me away. Living on the top floor is a special privilege. Mubarak doesn't seem to have any family. He comes from far away and doesn't tell anyone where. I'm sure that behind his forced smile this old man is hiding a dark history and even darker intentions. It's clear from what he says that he loves money and nothing else.

Where are you from? he asks me. Why aren't you married? What do you do? Where are your family?

I've become one of those people who doesn't care about anything, however important, but Mubarak's questions make me angry. I don't understand why he's so inanely inquisitive about me. I went out on the balcony and left him. He stared at the woman presenting the news, adjusting his glasses on his nose and sighing. Finally he shut up for a while and stopped talking bullshit to me.

Mubarak came up to me the first time I went into the café he owns. Welcome amongst us, he said, You're like a son to me. He said that and other things that sounded like cheap attempts to ingratiate himself. We agreed I could order drinks on account and pay at the end of the month. After that there was nothing said between us. The only regulars at the café are some retirees and a few has-beens on whom life has turned its back. The café's very close to the apartment so I'm not thinking of going to any other one. Sometimes I pick up a cup of coffee and bring it back to the apartment. He's morbidly inquisitive and sticks his nose into the asses of those around him without good cause. I try to ignore the looks he gives me—he and the insolent people around him. I go in and pore over a newspaper, though I have no desire to read any of the stories. One day one of them followed me to the bus stop and I managed to shake him off. I gathered from their conversations that he was an informer or a lackey for some government agency. Mubarak is the only one who's dared to knock on my door so far. How did he know which apartment it was? He said that, since I was alone and out of work, he was offering to let me be his partner in some project he didn't disclose. If we succeed in it (he said "we," plural), you'll be a king, he said. As for himself, he claimed he had so little time left to live that he didn't have any such aspirations. What he said didn't make me curious to find out what it was he thought would make me a king. He's a big talker, probably suspect, and I should be wary of him. A king? In practice that goes way beyond my aspirations, which are absurdly limited, for which I deserve a special dose of pity. Anyway, I'm a filthy slave that no one knows or cares for, and that suits me fine. That creature finally tired of me, turned off the television and left. He did say goodbye, but I didn't respond. I saw him limp into the square. He stopped a while and then walked off, full of confidence. I didn't ask him why he was limping, but I'm pretty sure that his glasses are just part of a disguise. Everything about him is suspicious, even his smile.

In the building opposite me a teenage girl often looks out at me in my long night sessions. She looks at me, waves her hand, and holds up her phone, suggesting that I give her my number and that she's alone and available. Sometimes I ignore her and sometimes I respond with a smile that goes to waste in the darkness. I couldn't possibly make the foolish mistake of seducing an immature girl like her, but I'm reluctant to claim any virtue, even to myself. I want to live invisibly, unseeable even as a reflection. Her balcony is closed and I'm still waiting. I don't know what draws me to her. I'm not so hungry that I'm going to break my long and voluntary abstinence from women with any old piece of meat that invites in anyone who comes up to her. Yet I do find myself inquisitive, even intrigued. Aren't I cured of being interested in anything? I'll get sick again. The balcony that I've been interested in recently seems dark and unpromising. Why the hell am I so stubborn? A few days ago she threw a piece of paper off her balcony. I interrupted my seclusion and slowly went down to pick it up. My heart was racing. It was a small piece of paper, folded and scented, and her phone number was written on it in pink ink. I took it home, even more interested in her balcony. When she watched me pick up the piece of paper, I didn't sign to her that I didn't have a phone. A phone's a luxury I can do without and, besides, I can't afford to buy another one just so that our heartbeats can meet halfway between one ring and another. I'm as broke as a gambler who's lost his shirt. Is she in love with me? I avoid asking myself this question.

Tonight it was an ordeal breaking free from the old man. I sat on the balcony pretending to myself that I wasn't looking forward to her looking out at me. The little tart teases me by going missing some nights. My book remained unopened on the small table in front of me. I felt as listless and apathetic as a castrated bull. I had a powerful expectation that she would do me harm in some way. I wouldn't be her first victim, or her last. I would just be a male who marked his presence between her thighs, like many others before and after. She might be really passionate, frustrated and desirous, but who falls in love with a shadow and looks forward to meeting it? She had created an image of me in her imagination without even seeing my face in detail. I'm a night creature most of the time, and the night is a playground for desire, a fertile pasture for every hungry imagination. My own imagination is depleted and dried up. I don't like to feel sorry for myself, and I'm no good at doing it in the first place. My history with women is embarrassing. I have no experience and the only thing in me that has changed since I was a teenager is that I'm now burned out, just ashes.

It's three o'clock in the morning. The weather's a little cold but I'm on fire watching for her silhouette to appear. I was about to have a shower to punish my body for disobeying me at a time when I needed it to be obedient, but at the last minute I was too lazy to bother. My weak will is my chronic defect. Inane rambling. I'll close the balcony shutters and go to sleep. I haven't gone down to the café for a week, but I might try to do so tomorrow if I can. I remember Mubarak. The fact that he came to see me was like advance notice of a night as ugly as his face. The light on the balcony opposite hasn't come on for me and I haven't read anything. No great loss as far as I'm concerned. What really worries me, though, is that I'm interested in her and I'm waiting for tomorrow. I slipped under the bedding to die a little death. My head's heavy on the pillow, and I wish it had been cut off in that incident in the past. In that case I'd now be up above laughing at the fates that have deprived me of my fair share in life.

Everyone who heard about that incident told me later that I was nearly killed. I have a different perspective on it now, and time has a tendency to correct what people say. I won another chance at life but I wouldn't say I've made good use of it. It was a chance that others, the people consumed by that vicious war, would have made better use of. Those people were offered as sacrifices to the gods. In that decade of fire and tears, each faction killed the guilty and the innocent without distinction as a way to win the favor of their bloody gods, whether they were rebel commanders in the mountains with their morbid beliefs or government soldiers who wanted to win promotion by trampling on the bodies of the dead. O the religion of God! God alone knows how many sacrificial victims disappeared or were killed and never heard of again, or which god devoured them. Some other teenagers and I were abducted from the corner of the main street in our village, there in Serdj El Ghoul north of Sétif. It was devastating for my family. Time would heal that, as it always does, but I came closer to death than at any other time in my life. A man who was working with the death squads didn't know that and he saved me from them when he recognized me, but that just put me on track for another kind of death. Many years later I was sitting in a pizzeria on Rue Hassiba in Algiers when I saw my savior come in. His body had plumped out and his jowls had drooped. My appearance had changed too and he didn't remember me. It's enough that he recognized me in that forest when everything was hazy. Throughout my only night as an abductee I was tied up and blindfolded. I pissed in my pants from the fear and the cold, constantly muttering all the short Quranic verses I could remember. Until dawn I prayed to God to save me and I stopped praying only when I heard the metal door open. I concluded that those people were stronger than anyone and that God had abandoned me. On the edge of the valley, in the forest of death, they took off my blindfold. The man was from our village. He shouted in their faces. He's a secondary school kid and had nothing to do with anything, he said. In the pizzeria I stood up and embraced the middle-aged man he had become. I reminded him of the incident. It was the first time I had hugged anyone with such affection and felt such gratitude toward someone. After everything I went through after my "escape" from death, I now wonder which of us is indebted to the other. He paid for my sandwich, gave me some spending money, and left. I was in a really pitiable state, although the most difficult part was yet to come. My aunt had died a few days earlier. After the condolence rituals were done, I didn't wait for her children to tell me I was now surplus to needs. I forgive them. I too feel I'm superfluous wherever I go. She put up with me in her house for many years when I came to her fleeing from death and I decided not to go on taking advantage of her, whether she was alive or dead. I passed my baccalaureate exams and went to university thanks to her. Death puts an end to everything. I saw her as a substitute for my mother. She was strict with her children but she always treated me differently.

My memories of my mother are distant and hazy. I feel no emotional attachment to her. Sometimes I think I was born without a mother, that I was born instead from my father's back when he was watering the fields. It wasn't long before my father joined her. He loved me with a love that had no equal, but it was clear that he loved her more than he loved me, because he followed her and abandoned me and my brother Ammar. My aunt hadn't had any sons and saw me as her opportunity to have one. She pampered me to an extraordinary extent and I didn't disappoint her. I played my role in a way that would have suited an only son. Her daughters were envious of me and sometimes they would hit me. They were much older than me. I often snooped on them when they were washing or changing their clothes. I lived out roles that were not mine, standing in for people who were dead or missing, or had never been born. I was an interloper, living an incidental life. Then my aunt died. The doctor's report said it was a heart attack but I knew I had killed her off with the curse that I carry with me. I'm good at killing off the people that love me. Loving me is a sure recipe for a quick death. Where's the love I carried in my heart for all those who gave me their unlimited love? I stopped visiting the grave of my maternal aunt and before that my father's grave and that of my paternal aunt, although I was like her substitute son. How's my brother Ammar? We saw each other a few years ago at the funeral of my maternal aunt. He said he missed me and I should go back to Serdj El Ghoul. I miss him terribly now. I know he loves me and I haven't done right by him. But I've lost contact with him in his own interest because his life is more important to me than my own life, and I don't want him to try his luck with that curse that I carry.

Is it as crowded and annoying up above as it is for us here? I imagine that up above there's a hall where they display all the inevitabilities that shaped our lives and the possible and probable destinies of all those who have lived on earth.

I can hear the old man shouting, talking to people only he can see. He scolds them for dying too soon, argues with old neighbors, and tells his late wife he has to get up early to do something, something different every time. The poor man is senile and has started to have dementia. I'll never forget what his son Mourad did for me, yet I still think he's a bastard. He paid a woman to look after his father, then went off and left him alone. I've lived without a father for years. I go to the old man's apartment and he disgusts me with his slobber, he says the most unexpected things and makes up strange sentences that I don't understand. I think they stem from a mixture of imagination and reality, the past that he wanted but that never came about and the bleak present that he never expected. I feel sorry for him. Sometimes he calls me Mourad and in return I try to repay the debt. His son gave me the apartment to live in without me having to pay him a penny. The old man fought in the War of Independence, but I don't know how he obtained two flats in the same building. They're part of a project into which the government shoves all the rats and their families and gives them ownership. This country is a big trick. I can't sleep when I hear him shouting. This miserable old man deserves a merciful death, and a week ago I seriously thought of slipping something into his food, but then I backed off. I was too hard-hearted to inflict such mercy on a weak man like him. Mourad deserves to be executed at the stake. He didn't appreciate the blessing of having a father in his life and he went off to Germany. It's been more than a year since he's seen him. He used to call me once a month to check up on his father. He's a terrible actor and his voice gives him away. I suspect he wanted to hear that his father had died. He stopped asking after him completely six months ago.

I know the old man's life history. In my presence he brings up his distant, jumbled memories of poverty, his harsh childhood, and the Algerian war for independence. Sometimes he loses all his memory and he can't even remember his name, but he never forgets to pray. He's conscientious about that. Often he forgets that he's prayed, so he prays two or three times. He might miss one prostration or do one extra by mistake, and he usually does it without bothering to wash. I brought him an ablution stone that he can use as a substitute for abluting with water. A few days later I heard him speaking to Mourad on the phone at the top of his voice. He was angry and sad and he threw the stone at the television screen. I ran to him and hugged him. He was gasping like a child. I felt rather sorry for him and cursed my luck. But for some reason I didn't fully sympathize with him. I thought he'd been cruel and unfair in his life and deserved this end. Those were just ideas that I immediately forgot. I bought him another television that was bigger and more expensive and threw the ablution stone in the trash bin. As long as his heart's pure, he's in a fit state to pray, I thought. I leave him constantly watching the Quran channel. He likes the voice of Abdel Basit Abdel Samad more than anyone else's and his face beams when he hears him reciting. He's deeply religious, or he's trying to make up for the past. He reminds me of the Quran teacher in our village—similar features and the same dignity of old age. I remember rubbing clay on the wooden writing tablets to clean them, the inkwells, the reed pens, and the ink we made from burned wool. I expect that teacher's probably dead by now. I wasn't as mischievous as the other kids. I was slow-witted and apathetic and that annoyed him, and I don't think he liked me much. That was his good luck or else he would have died earlier, since anyone who likes me soon meets their demise. I forgive him all the beatings, which left the soles of my feet swollen, because God's word doesn't come free of charge. What has God's attitude toward me been recently?

Life doesn't accept the logic of substitute players, but that's how I am now as far as Mourad is concerned. He provides the lodging and I spend time with his father, as a guard, as a companion, as a substitute for Mourad. The old man comes to his senses sometimes and is fully aware that his son has abandoned him and that I'm not Mourad. I suspect he deliberately calls me by his son's name even when he's in his right mind and his memory's working. He understood the deal, and maybe he's come to terms with the new situation. I have also realized that his son treated me despicably, for which I'm very grateful to him. I lock the old man in so that he doesn't go out and lose his way in the streets. I protect him from any intruders, pay the water and electricity bills, supervise the woman who looks after the house, and pay her salary every month. There's less than one month left of the year we agreed. I'm grateful to my friend in a way. He took me on as a guard dog without telling me in advance and without me having any prior qualifications. My sense of smell is weak but my hearing's very sharp. My money's run out and I've been through some hard times in this house. In fact I sometimes found nothing to eat and I couldn't afford soap to wash with. Because of my conscience I did face one stupid moral dilemma. I'm not a thief, but some problems call for urgent solutions of one kind or another. I once called a taxi and dragged the old man to the nearest post office to withdraw his pension as a fighter in the War of Independence. His balance had accumulated. Mourad was the only other person who had the authority to withdraw the money and I discovered it was a fortune compared with my own means. I bought him some sheep's liver and cooked it and we ate together. He looked as happy as a child, and I celebrated my victory over my conscience with some bottles of beer. A dirty insect fell inside one of them. I got rid of it, then poured what was left in the bottle down my throat as if nothing had happened. I found I had to sell my books to the booksellers at the square near the central post office in order to make ends meet. I had spent the last dinar of the money I had raised by selling my laptop earlier. I didn't have anything else I could sell without embarrassment. I decided to take a share of the old man's pension. Free lodging isn't fair compensation for spending so much time with him. Mourad tricked me and I should have changed the agreement to make it fairer. Besides, dogs don't make good guards when they're hungry.

Who am I to judge others? Mourad was rash and reckless, yet I still see him as good, in a way. But if one had to look at it from another angle and describe him properly, he's a womanizer. I don't doubt that the bed I sleep in has been visited by a host of passing women. Underneath it I found a bra and in my second month here the doorbell rang and I opened it to find an ugly woman in her forties asking after him. He didn't spare any female and his taste is disgusting. A case of aesthetic blindness. He spent most of his father's pension on them and when he'd gone as far as he could with them here he moved on to abroad. He'll probably die between a woman's legs. I now live as a monk in what used to be a den of debauchery. He sold his car and paid a large bribe to someone in the German embassy to get him a visa. Later he told me he was very happy: he could sleep with countless women with blue eyes and smooth white legs, none of them with armpits that smell bad. He avoids any accusation that he has been negligent toward his father, though that's a well-established fact. He cried a lot in our last phone conversation and said he wasn't going to have any children so that he wouldn't impose on anyone the burden of looking after him when he grows old. I think he's made a final decision and he won't be father or son to anyone other than himself. He pissed on the past and everything about it and left. I found the apartment was a shambles—dust, leftover food, empty beer cans, and rat shit. I'm not easily disgusted. Once I spent several nights in a shack right next to a dumpster full of trash. I spoke to him and he told me he no longer felt attached to the place and I had to deal with it. He came back that night, kissed his father on the forehead, and asked him to forgive him. That was when I knew for certain he would never come back. His last week here he was off with a woman, telling her that of all the women he knew she was the closest to his heart. They went to Oran and he promised he would help arrange for her to join him in Germany. As we stood talking at the door, she asked me if Mourad had asked me to tell her anything, and I said no. She called him a bastard and left.

The old man calmed down at dawn and stopped shouting. The cleaning woman would come again in the morning. I had received her wages for a whole year from Mourad. I don't like to add to the sacrifices of others. She's a hard-working woman who works like a robot without making a noise. She greets me sullenly and is almost mute in my presence, but I sometimes hear her exchanging words with the old man. She cleans his apartment daily, and my apartment whenever I ask her to, and I rely on her to buy everything we need. I've become a substitute for Mourad and so she has to obey me. For my part I don't overwork her and I think she's accepted the situation. She's a pleasant creature but there's something slavish in her nature. I doubled her wages and she didn't seem especially grateful. It's expensive to live in isolation but I don't pay her from my own pocket. She lives near to this neighborhood and her presence is vital for me and for him. She's honest and she's bringing up her children alone. Women like her will be extinct in a few years' time. My drowsiness disappeared and I went off to the balcony again. Further evidence of how attached I am to that bitch. Day broke: that meant I wouldn't be seeing a faint light on her balcony, though even that might not have sent anything more than a misleading signal. I'll have to wait for tonight. Damn waiting!

2

Scramble

I WAS RIGHT WHEN I predicted that life would save me up till it found a big shithole to dump me in. Damn my luck and damn the old man, the son of a bitch. And damn the public slaughterhouse where I've been standing for hours. I hate the smell of medicine and the sight of doctors and nurses with faces as blank as those of vets treating animals. I go out to the square and come back. I can't stay away from him for long. He keeps calling me, I mean calling Mourad, and I'm the substitute dog that has to play the role of Mourad till the end. This hospital, a legacy of colonialism, is almost unchanged from the time it was built. They've added some annexes to it, mutilating it irreparably. It's crowded Rouïba Hospital, Rouïba, and its industrial area. They should execute those people in public, those major-league grifters. His condition deteriorated and I brought him here. But I've grown tired of waiting beside him all the time. He might need a companion if they decide to admit him for a few days. Never mind, I'll sort it out. The doctor asked me if he's been eating well and I told him without out thinking that he'd lost his appetite. I lied to him. All the food we had has run out. Sometimes he'd have to go without food till nighttime. Then I'd give him a little food with some sweetened water. I was hungry too. I spent the last dinar I had, and when he fell seriously ill I was worried about taking him to the post office. He couldn't go out without running a risk. I wouldn't take that risk, so we were stuck.

Slaves rebel at the first opportunity. The woman abandoned us after the first week I couldn't pay her. I came around to the idea of selling the television. It's a big one and it's the latest model. I started fantasizing about the amount of money I could raise with it. When the time came I got a third of what we had paid. It might be stolen, the man said, exploiting my need for money. As for the man in the electronic appliances store, he yelled in my face and threatened to call the police if I went into his store again, on the grounds that he didn't deal in stolen goods. I took the money home with the feeling that I was just a piece of bird shit on the roof of the world. A wind might blow up and throw me out into the great void. Why not? I was a little happy nonetheless. I hired a taxi and went home with some vegetables, meat, and bags of large diapers, and had some money left to pay the woman. It had been an unforgettable week and it looked like it would cast its pall over the days to come as well. I've experienced all kinds of disgusting things before, but taking off someone's diapers, getting rid of the shit and piss, and putting on another one pushes the limits when it comes to humiliation. Diapers are the most important invention in history. As for my inordinate humaneness, that's a historical mistake that keeps recurring. The doctor tells me, totally relaxed, that old age is incurable. A great start! Maybe he thought I wanted the old man to recover and escape death! He needs to do some tests. Can you do them here? Some of the equipment in the lab is out of order and won't be repaired any time soon. You can try a private lab. Long live the Algerian state, the welfare state with stuffed pockets. All that's left in my pocket is a 2,000-dinar note and that won't be much good. I wish he would die. Why is he hanging on to life? The matter will be left undecided till tomorrow, or forever. I was sweating heavily, my clothes were dirty, and I wanted to go home for a shower. My greatest achievement today was that they decided to admit him to the hospital. I had wanted to beg the scowling doctor to inject him with something that would make him sleep a long time, a sleep like death, a deep coma. I wouldn't have protested. On the contrary, I would have been grateful to see his hellish face, which makes him look like a murderer anyway.

What need did I have for freedom? That's a question I posed, belatedly and with not a little remorse, on the same night I decided to win back my freedom at any cost. I hadn't done anything wrong and I wasn't sick. I was sure of myself and that was enough. I tricked them into believing I was sick, in order to save myself, and I fell into more damned trouble. I don't want to go over the incident or say why I found myself forced to cower in a mental hospital like a patient that's not expected to recover. That's nothing to do with anyone else; it's a secret between me and my fate. As for my memories of the people in white coats, most of them are unpleasant. I've never hated anyone so much as doctors and lawyers, the false symbols of humanity. I put on an act for some of them and tricked them for a good long time. I played dominoes with them and they didn't begrudge me their cigarettes. Most of them graduated from university as damaged goods and their competence is permanently in doubt. That helped me later, although they destroyed me with drugs in the beginning. I'll curse them till I die. I lied to a fat nurse and told her she was attractive. People who are frustrated will believe even a madman. I showered her with endless compliments and gained amazing privileges. A little flattery works wonders. The doctor revealed to me that he was going to write me a letter to the effect that I had completely recovered. I was going to regain my reason through a certificate from him, but my freedom was in the balance. When darkness fell I headed to the doctor's office. He had signed my release paper and I found him lying back in his chair because of the heat and the broken air-conditioning. The working conditions didn't suit him and he was thinking of emigrating. He didn't want to be a slave to a state that sucked his blood. That's what he told me, and he spoke to me just like he would to any sane friend of his. He showed me the release paper and I tried to show a little interest. He put it back in my file. I took my leave and left. I agreed with the nurse that I would never go back to the big ward. I would escape that night. Her face looked really sad. Inside I felt sorry for her and I promised I would marry her. We'll be together forever my love, I said, and she believed me. If it hadn't been for her, getting out of that damned place would have been impossible. The hospital management was meant to inform some government department the next day, so that they could take me back to somewhere I didn't deserve to be, but I had different ideas. I had memorized the layout of the hospital inch by inch in advance. My girlfriend took on the task of covering my absence, while I slipped into a place that wouldn't occur to anyone and hid there. At dawn I had a new appointment with freedom.

I've put a new diaper on him and given him some water to drink. He might spend the night alone. But I'm happy to get out of the hospital unburdened. I can't stay the night with him. I don't have an ID card or any other document that would prove my identity, and the hospital staff needs proof of identity for people who stay with the patients. In the morning, as I was taking him to the hospital in the *Protection Civile* ambulance, the cleaning woman told me her teenage son could stay the night with him. It was an admirable solution, for which I expressed my gratitude, until she told me in an almost imperious tone that I would have to pay him. I tried to bargain with her, saying she would have one less stomach to fill morning and evening. The boy would eat his share of the hospital food and the poor old man's share, but she refused. I agreed of course. I would pay him for two nights in advance and send him over as soon as I got back. Five hundred dinars a night was a good deal. That was the best available. In fact it was all I could afford.

Mourad wouldn't be very interested in his father's condition. He'd cope with his short-lived sadness by having a woman and a few drinks, then end up coming to terms with the idea of his father's imminent demise. Yet I had to tell him. I'd kept the last number he called me from in a small notebook but I couldn't remember where I'd put it. There was still the problem of finding a phone, but I would find a way. How I wished a miracle would happen and I would find Mourad standing right in front of me so that I could kick him in the ass. The bastard. I don't hate him. I'm just angry, but I still feel grateful to him. He took me in to exploit me and salve his conscience, but I'm still very grateful, even after everything I've suffered with his father, and not just a little grateful. As far as I'm concerned, his shirts, trousers, and underwear also count in his favor. When I first tried them on I found they didn't fit. He was fat and I looked like a real clown in them. I went to a tailor nearby and he adjusted them to fit me. Nothing in life has ever been my size: my life is like a patchwork garment. I need a tailor who can reshape my life the way I want it. What do I really want? Maybe to discard life and face death as naked as I was when I came from the void in the first place. I had a difficult choice to make and I could have neglected the old man till he died and his corpse stank. I could have gone away and never come back, or come back after his story was forgotten. I didn't. In my heart I felt just as sorry for him as I would have felt for my own father if he had been destined to live long enough for me to see him as an old man. The bus shakes and smells foul. I can't bear the way I smell either. My father died and one of the distant consequences of that is that this senile man has found someone to look after him. I've shouted in his face, I've insulted him and cursed him because of his son, but I haven't abandoned him. I'm not a complete bastard. When he dies soon, as I hope he will, I'll gradually forget about my complaints about his excretions and their smell, which cling to me and to his apartment, which I have to clean when I go back and relax a little. I'll ask God to have mercy on him. Fate gave me a chance to see firsthand the state my father might eventually have reached. A wise man prefers to die in good health. Weakness in old age is humiliating to those who can't find anyone to look after them.

I reached the station and got off the horrible bus without paying the conductor, a smart-ass young man who failed to notice me. I walked off as if I didn't have a care in the world. It's not the first time I've done that. The feel of the green 2,000-dinar note between my fingers gives me vigor and a sense of power. I'll break it and keep half for the maid's son, after buying a packet of Rym cigarettes, some soap for the shower, and a SIM card to call Mourad. I won't promise my stomach a meal. A strong coffee will do. I'm hungry but I can take it. I'll be happy as long as the hunger doesn't keep me awake at night. This will be the first night I've gone back to sleep in my own apartment after spending a week staying up with the old man. I can't say I hope he'll recover. The doctor said, There's no cure for old age, and I won't second-guess him in his area of expertise. I have two apartments and I can spend the night hungry in whichever one I want. Total luxury, but without a meal. An empty belly has no conscience, and a full belly even less so. I should have been on guard against that. I withdrew a considerable sum from the old man's pension and then I was extravagant. Before that, when I used to work as a porter in the wholesale stores in Oued Smar, I made loads of money but most of it went missing or was stolen from me. I cracked the skull and injured the shoulder of a porter who worked with me there, and then I ran away. Maybe I only had my suspicions about him, I don't know, but I was already full of anger toward him and the next time he provoked me it seemed like a good opportunity to act. Before I took my revenge and left, I asked the pig who employed us to give me back my ID card for some bureaucratic procedure, and I said I'd hand it back the next day. He kept hold of our ID cards in case of similar situations. He gave us free lodging but the food was on us, and no one could find me or find out where I was unless they had a photocopy of the card, but I don't think that guy, who had a beard like a devil's, had taken any precautions. His only concern was to buy nuts and honey at the end of every day to make himself more virile. What good would virility do him when he was such a pig?

I had some tough times, hiding away and starving. I slept in the bus station at El Kharrouba for several nights. A cleaner harassed me and only with difficulty did I manage to escape from the guards. It was only routine harassment but I couldn't go back there. Before that I'd thought of taking a bus to the desert, or to the west or east of the country, not to Sétif of course, but then I changed my mind. One moonlit night I reached a neighborhood close to the railway station at Rouïba. I don't know why I ended up there in particular. I was hungry and smelled foul. Finally I managed to have a shower and get rid of the smell. Mourad happened to be passing by and we had a long conversation of which I remember nothing. He was half-drunk, while I hadn't had any food in my stomach for a day and a night. He agreed I could sleep at his place and told me he might let me stay longer once he checked the next day that I wasn't wanted by the police. Fortunately my name wasn't on the wanted list. My ID card fell into the toilet at the station and got wet. I fished it out, but when I found it was completely ruined, I threw it back in and poured a bucket of water over it. I'd forgotten my name when he asked me about it the first time. I had been giving myself a different name everywhere I went. I was very hungry and he fed me. That day I had gone around the shopkeepers and cheap restaurants but they chased me away and none of them offered me a hot meal. I would have been prepared to burn the whole city down if I'd had a chance. Does anyone out there know what it feels like to be hungry and begging when people refuse to feed you? Throughout the time I lived with him, I called Mourad my friend. At first he was annoyed, since I was just a dirty homeless guy, lost and always hungry. Yet I won his heart and he accepted me as his equal in some ways. Maybe he saw me as a gift from fate, a gift he found by chance near the garbage dump.

In the middle of the week another intruder visited me around noon. He pressed the doorbell, which was out of order, and then knocked on the door. I saw him through the peep hole. He had a full beard and was wearing a yellow cloak. I'm always wary of people who dress ostentatiously. His face wasn't completely unfamiliar to me, as I'd seen him before. He had been following me with his eyes that morning and I had ignored him. That was when I went to the café very early and had breakfast on account. I made nice to Mubarak, smiling at him for the first time. I needed him to lend me some money, any amount, on the grounds that his neighbor, the poor old man, was ill. I wanted to appeal to his better nature but he's a big bastard, and I didn't get anything out of him. I was pathetic, and anyone, believer or sinner, would have pitied me. The man who was watching me in the café kept stroking his neatly trimmed beard with his right hand. Now he was doing exactly the same thing on the other side of the door, as he waited for it to open. He gave me a smile and said, I've come to visit the old man. I heard he was very ill. (Who told him?) I'm the imam of the mosque in our neighborhood, the Takoua mosque, if you don't recognize me, the imam continued. This old man is a believer and a great freedom fighter. He used to pray right behind me in the front row and he'd never miss a prayer time.

Was he praising him or finding fault with him for staying away from prayers? Besides, when was all this? I hadn't seen him leave the apartment since the time I arrived. He'd been abandoned by his son and was waiting to die, nothing more. The imam started praying for him and I expected him to put his hand in his pocket and take out some money. The old man was hungry and words alone don't silence an empty stomach. Finally he slipped me some money and I felt guilty for thinking ill of him as a man of God. But the worst of my earlier suspicions were confirmed when he revealed the real reason for his visit. He assumed an earnest expression and laid out his proposal to me. In fact it sounded like some kind of scam. I'm someone who's permanently vulnerable to scams: that's nothing new and not really anything to feel sorry about. He wanted me to let him bring clients to the apartment for "sharia exorcisms." I could have half of what he earned—word of honor between us—and unlimited blessings. I agreed, almost without thinking. I hadn't had a beer for many days and necessity is the mother of depravity. We agreed on a time, and he said he had plenty of custom-ers. The faithful protect their brothers, and I would have to vacate my apartment, he added. I also agreed to that. I would stay in the old man's apartment. It would be best if you kept away longer, he said, trying hard to keep me out of the way. Muslims should keep their word, okay. He scowled when I asked how much one of these sessions cost. The people are sick and they pay generously to get rid of the devil and make room for the angels lurking inside them to reappear, he said. The spiritual procedure is very time-consuming. You won't be too put out, he assured me. It would just be two or three times a week in the afternoon, and sometimes daily. I agreed again. Poverty knows no morals and this religious man was going to throw poverty out of the apartment. In the mental hospital I was convinced I was sane, and just put-ting on an act for them without believing in the act myself. As for the state I'm in these days, it's worth reconsidering. Circumstances impose on us new rules for engaging with life all the time, and one has to adapt. A dark area in my mem-ory refuses to remind me of what happened. I relived my unfortunate experience in the form of horrible nightmares for months on end but finally I managed to forget, or else I would have killed myself. Death through cowardice is easier to bear than facing the pain when you are completely defenseless. I'm not sad I've forgotten what happened, and even if I did remember, it would still be a secret that I would take with me to the grave. And work together in righteousness, the imam concluded, then withdrew without further ado. I was left thinking, unable to back out of the agreement. Life never ceases to come up with predicaments and with them freedom of choice becomes a distant luxury. An hour later he brought his first customer. My apartment stank. It hadn't been cleaned for a week, but I didn't have anything to be ashamed of. Besides, cleanliness is in the heart, and preparing the apartment for him hadn't been part of the agreement in the first place. He was surprised when he saw the state it was in, but I ignored his grumbling as if it were nothing to do with me. He finished his inspection, said he needed an hour or more, and asked me to leave. I started waiting for the end of the exorcism, spending half the first hour in the café, which was empty. It was a hot, humid day. Mubarak took me aside and said he was sorry he couldn't lend me the money I had asked for. But he said he would drop in on me at home that evening. I left his place and stood in the shade for a while. Where should I go for the rest of the hour we had agreed? At the entrance to the building I met some women: two of them went in while an older woman stayed in the taxi that had brought them. Before long the taxi left, to come back and take the two women later. I went back to counting the minutes and from the square I could hear the old man shouting. The prostate pain is unbearable, he was saying. He held out for a while, suppressing his pains. But when the pain got the better of him he shouted out again. This time he was calling Mourad at the top of his voice. I went upstairs. Then he chose to be patient and a cautious silence prevailed. Suddenly there was another sound from my apartment. I hesitated a while, quite a long while in fact. The money in my pocket kept me silent, but something was bugging me inside. I felt sorry for the imam's patient, though she did have a companion to help her with the difficult situation and help the imam against the djinn that possessed her. It's not at all easy to drive out djinn that have taken up residence in the body of a somewhat plump young woman, and even in her black hijab she projected more than enough allure to excite a troupe of devils. At the entrance to the building she had walked past me. I looked down, away from her, but I noticed half a smile on her lips. I pretended to be modest by looking down, while the devil found plenty of scope to play in my heart.

More minutes passed and the sounds from my apartment began to sound suspicious. The djinn had started panting, following the lead of the humans inside. I could hear mutterings and muffled words, and that something was bugging me more and more. Might it have been my conscience? I had had the foresight to disable the lock on the inside of the door. I stood for some moments in the narrow corridor between the front doors of the two apartments, and then I pushed the door of my apartment with all my weight. The woman who had been leaning on it to keep it shut fell to the floor on the inside. I burst into the room and was amazed to see the dignified imam, a man in his fifties, stretched out on my bed naked, while the woman who had been wearing the black hijab now had a blue nightshirt tight around her flabby body. She was smiling broadly this time and pretended to be surprised, but not very convincingly.

Fate overcomes everyone. This is a fact I won't let anyone debate with me from now on. For example, this filthy apartment was fated to be a den of debauchery, whoever lived in it, and I was fated to be always deprived. I didn't celebrate the money the imam had given me for long. I hated the fact he had deceived me, and I punished him. I gave him and his two cows a few kicks. She's my second wife, he said, The first doesn't know and I don't have anywhere to be alone with her in a sharia-compliant way. That's how my imam justified his position. He likes to use the word "sharia" in every other sentence. I'm not shocked by him. He ended up giving me some more money so I was rather pleased, and I still had the option of blackmailing him. My plans for the night included preparing a banquet for myself and the old man. I overlooked the fact that he needed the doctor and medicine and decided to set aside what I had left of the money to pay the electricity bill and buy some cans of beer. Selfishness, poor judgment, I didn't have time for regrets. In the afternoon I was visited by a guy who persuaded me to hand over most of the sum and left. It was the guy with the bookstore who sits in the café sometimes and uses complicated words. My debts had mounted up and were over the limit we'd agreed. He deducted the amount I owed and dashed my hopes of getting beer from him on credit in the future. Pay what you owe and order what you want. That was the new rule he set in his dealings with me. His face was implacable and there was no way I could negotiate. Defeated by fate yet again, I left. I had hoped for a night when the old man would have his fill of meat and I would get drunk and watch the balcony for the silhouette of the girl whose flirting I now found tedious. But now those hopes were dashed. I ended up having eggs and cheese for dinner and nothing on the balcony but cigarettes.

The balcony opposite was closed. It had been closed for many nights, and I had almost given up hope of her coming out again. I wondered if there was any point in waiting for the balcony light to come on and her silhouette to appear. I always plow the impossible and reap nothing of value. Ten o'clock came and nothing new. I looked in on the old man every half hour. It was raining, a miserable night. I cheered up, however, when I remembered that Mubarak hadn't kept his appointment with me, but like anything that gives me pleasure it didn't last long. Several minutes later he was seated in the sitting room, soaked and unusually silent. I was about to ask about the local imam, but I didn't really want to. I took the initiative this time. What do you want of me, I asked. In a remote and abandoned cemetery in the part of the country where he came from, he said, bands of bad guys had buried a real treasure during the civil war. In the days of banditry and gangs that roamed by night, people paid ransoms and the money piled up. But cash wasn't safe and gold alone is always king. There were some buried ingots there, and so we had to dig up what must be the most valuable grave in the world, thirty-four ingots. Few people were aware of this and the army had killed some of them, and only this dubious old man knew the exact location of the grave and he'd be the only heir. I need a young man, he told me, and there's no one suitable but you, we only need to spend two nights there, when there's a full moon. We'll have to dig deep, there are shepherds in the area and people no longer bury their dead in that cemetery. We'd be easily visible in the daylight, so we'll have to do it at night. The hardest work will fall to you. Your share will be one third and an extra ingot as a gift. We'll finish the job before we go together to the nearest town. I'll tell you the name of the town when we agree. I'll come back to Rouïba and you can disappear into the capital forever. Also it would be preferable if you don't come back as I don't know where your family is. Be careful, forget your Mubarak, and live like a king.

I've no idea what kind of pills he'd taken before coming to see me. I listened to him and interrupted him a few times to seek clarification, as if I were actually interested in his offer. Just out of curiosity. He gave me high hopes, if the mission succeeded, and he was fully confident it was a foregone conclusion I would agree. He stuck his hand in his pocket. He was carrying a large amount of money. I thought it would be an advance payment, but the man was cunning. I'm a hungry

27

puppy and he only has to show me a piece of bread for me to follow him. He left straight away. Why didn't I settle the matter at the time? That something inside me had stopped bugging me and had tempted me to embark on an adventure through which I could deal my fate a deadly blow.

3

Transparency

I'M HOSTAGE TO A BUNCH of circumstances and I can't see a logical reason why they should have picked on me rather than anyone else. I feel like a mouse strung up by its balls. The neighborhood's had no water in the taps for days and the apartment's in a terrible state. The shit's piling up in the toilet and I didn't want to grab a bucket and go begging for water. I did bring one bucketful of water from the café at dawn, but it's not enough at all. The sewer rats are cleaner than I am now. The neighbors took precautions by installing cisterns in case of a crisis, but I'm using the toilets in the mosque or in Mubarak's café, and now I have to act nice to him by smiling. The old man is asleep nearby. He just lies on a long sofa all day, and I move him to his bed if he gets tired. I won't lie and say that I don't hate him more than I did. I deliberately don't give him much to eat so that I don't have to change his diaper every hour. He had diarrhea and I seriously thought of arranging a quick death, so that I could regain my dignity. I gave him some medicine and luckily he improved. Then I was indescribably happy when he had constipation. Unfortunately it didn't last long. I've given him endless amounts of chocolate, the cheap kind of course. After that I came up with a less expensive solution, and rice became our staple diet. I'm the meek version of Mourad, a submissive dog rather than a rabid one roaming all over the place. I'm no one, just what people have wanted me to be. It was a waste of effort buying the SIM card and tracking down someone willing to lend me their phone to use for a few minutes. The last number he called from is no longer his, as far as I can see. A woman answered me. From her voice she sounded old and she spoke German. Many attempts over three days, and the same woman answered. A thousand curses on the rabid dog. I wanted to lure him into coming back, saying your father's dying and he wants to see you, don't deprive him of one last look. I was going to tell him every lie in the book and leave the place as soon as he came back. In a dream I had he did come back and his father didn't die, but that was just a figment of my imagination. By cutting off all links, he seems to have taken precautions for a possible moment of weakness that he expected to come.

The old man didn't stay long in the hospital. The cleaning woman's son went off with his mother and stopped spending the night with him. The doctor allowed him to be discharged and I brought him back reluctantly. I had set aside some money that would have saved me from begging for two weeks or more. The government had given the cleaning woman a place in social housing. The young man told me he'd been born in a rough neighborhood on the edge of the city and lived there for sixteen years. He was born and grew up like a rat in the shanties, and then they moved to live in one of those concrete boxes. I feel handicapped without that woman. She took care of cleaning the two apartments, and did the laundry and the shopping. They'd been moved to a remote area. Now I have to look after the old man. He came out of the hospital and went back to his apartment, not to anywhere else—the cemetery for example. I wonder if I'll cling to life like him when I grow old. She came to say goodbye to us. I think she felt some affection for us, sympathy or I don't know what. I feel nothing toward any human being. I forgave her for being mean when she left us earlier. She told me she felt like the old man was her father, and maybe I believed her. I was too old to be her son, yet I was a little saddened that we were going to lose her maternal protection. The old man and I were just two grown-up orphans. She volunteered to cook us one last meal. It was delicious, more delicious than the food she had cooked for us earlier. It tasted of real love. She said she wouldn't be able to work for us from now on. Her new home was too far away. But she planned to visit us from time to time and she apologized for leaving us on our own. You're nice, she told me, and she urged me not to let the old man die alone. I was frustrated and maybe I felt a little grateful toward her, but I forgot her five minutes after she left.

I wondered how I would deal with the new situation. I can't challenge even an ant, and I don't want to anyway. I hope he dies soon and I promise I'll be sad for him, as if he were very dear to my heart. Do I really hate him? I've moved the television from my apartment to his apartment. He sits stockstill in front of it all day long, dozing off and then waking up. He prays seated because he can no longer stand up by himself. Then he goes back to watching everything that's broadcast, with interest and sometimes with delight. He laughs for no reason, even at the weather forecast, and sometimes he thinks the newsreader is addressing him or asking him a question, so he answers and gets into a serious discussion in his booming voice. His voice has lost none of its strength, even when he was in the hospital. Another world. As for me, I laugh sometimes, though that's pathetic. Nothing works any longer. People are nothing but memories.

I wish my memory could be wiped clean. People are sculpted by their experiences, and I'm just a shapeless, shoddy piece of sculpture, made of fragments, the creature of others and of the experiments they have carried out on me. I agreed to be a guard dog because I was a wreck. To be honest I didn't expect all this torment. I just wanted to stay away from people, keep my distance, and have fun waiting for death, not to become a dishcloth for other people's mistakes, which is what Mourad made of me. Okay, nothing about me is worth lamenting. I've lived life with all its constraints. I worked as a garbage collector for three years. For a homeless man like me, it meant nothing that I had been to university or that I was a human being. I was exploited by everyone who could exploit me. I almost forgot everything I had learned at university, and experience taught me lessons that were more durable. If you're a subcontracted garbage collector, someone else collects your salary and gives you only a part of it. I loaded the garbage onto donkeys in the narrow lanes of the casbah. I ate the remains of food I found in the garbage bins. I vomited the first time and then grew used to it. I forgot my dignity forever. Dignity means nothing when you're hungry. The instinct to survive is stronger. A subcontracted garbage collector rents a room with a dilapidated ceiling and walls and sleeps on a dirty mattress. I was more pragmatic than anyone else in the world. Countless human beings live off garbage and I was no better than them. I'm someone whose flesh thrived on garbage, on food that overfed rich people threw away in houses, restaurants, and hotels. The contents of every home's garbage bin reflect the social status of the people who live there. I would hurry to grab it before it was too far gone to be edible. Some of the workers came across money and valuables, but the most I ever found was leftover food, shoes that were falling apart, and discarded or unwanted trousers. Once I found a book about happiness. I threw it away immediately and went back to my room at dawn to masturbate over the image that was stuck in my mind—that of a housewife in her fifties. My life has always fed off other people's leftovers.

I ate expired cheese and rotten fruit. My stomach grew used to that and I acquired immunity. Sometimes my luck would come up with some fresh chicken or turkey liver or gizzards. I would hold a barbecue in my room from time to time and I noticeably put on weight. My luck seemed to be on the rise when I moved to work on a truck in the Ben Aknoun area, where there were hotels with bars. I started finding beer cans and wine bottles that weren't completely empty and some that were unopened. It began with cans of soda and ended with me overjoyed if fate granted me something that would help me through the long empty day. I had a special bag I slung over my shoulder for that purpose. Sometimes I'd come back with the bag full, assured of supplies for days. The friend and colleague closest to my heart would help me fill the bag, indifferent to the religious views of our other colleague. Could I have saved my friend but didn't? I was paralyzed as I watched the wheel of the truck crush his stomach. I saw him, his eyes popping out, and I may have detected half a smile on his lips. That prig held me responsible. He said I could have pulled the guy out and that the man had reached out his hand to me. I'm not sure. I envied my friend anyway. Deliverance came to him quickly and free of charge, like an unexpected gift. He smiled at me and reached out his hand to say goodbye or invite me to cleanse myself of life and join him. He was kind and wished me well. There's no messing around with luck, so I'll have to bide my time. The other workers all glared at me as if I had pushed him under the truck. Maybe they suspected me from the start. Just idiots—instead of demanding their rights and breaking out of their state of legalized slavery, they held me responsible for the accident as if I were a superhero in charge of defying the will of God. After that a sense of guilt seeped into me, as if I were a real murderer, and I had nightmares. I saw the same scene in different forms every time. That period passed with minimal damage and I went back to not caring—invisible, silent, biding my time. The poor guy died and then I decided to give up that kind of work forever. Working as a subcontracted garbage collector is not a job you have many regrets about when you give it up.

No one else will be destined to write a life story as squalid as mine, although it's all true. Some of the facts smell so strong that they would overpower any perfume, however expensive it might be. When was the last time I bought a bottle of perfume? I'm still grateful to the exploitative garbage collector who subcontracted his job to me—another stupid act of gratitude on my part. In the last two months of those three damned years I grew lazy and he found another wretch to replace me when I decided to go. He had a word with one of his relatives in the wholesale stores in Oued Smar and that relative of his recommended me to a rich merchant who was religiously conservative but in fact just a pig. I said goodbye to my shabby room and settled down comfortably in my new job despite the hard work. I was happy to be sure of a place to spend the night without fearing the ceiling would fall in on my head if it started raining. The warehouse where I and others spent the night was a real palace compared with my previous room, but I lost my freedom and with it the pleasure of sleeping alone and naked.

I was drinking, but not for any particular purpose. Out of curiosity to explore, and then out of habit, as an escape that was expensive but productive in a way. Through it I forgot I was me, and it saved me from feeling crushed inside. It was quite an ordeal finding alcohol and somewhere to drink, but I found it was worth the trouble. The pig hated me and held back some of the money he owed me. He patronized me, treated me as an idiot. He called me "the drunkard" and threatened to fire me, without actually doing so. I admit I deceived him for weeks. I couldn't avoid playing along with him and maybe I even wanted to reform myself, but it was a faint and intermittent desire. I frequented the nearby mosque and took part in Friday prayers. I had fasted regularly in the past but praying regularly was too much. My mind was exhausted, as was my body. Even so, never mind, I wasn't doing anyone any harm. On religious holidays I would stay on my own because my workmates went off to their families. I would have a break from them for two or three nights. On one occasion he caught me drinking in the warehouse. He laid into me and threw me out. The place where you make a living must never smell of the devil's brew, he told me. I plucked up my courage and went back an hour later to plead with him. I had nowhere else to go. I repeated to him something I had heard in the Friday sermon, that God forgives all sins, otherwise people would be helping Satan against their fellow Muslims. I promised I was repentant and he forgave me. After that he and the devil were on my case, and I realized that he agreed to take me back only because I was reliable, worked hard, and didn't ask for much.

I noticed the way they looked at me in the café, wary of the stranger that had suddenly landed among them. But I ignored them. At first it was annoying to be under constant surveillance, but then their curiosity wore off and I got used to it, just as I've got used to everything else in the past. My talents in this regard are extraordinary. Only that bookshop guy discovered that I drink; he's an expert in carousing and well aware of the signs. I exaggerate. I'm not literally a carouser. Once he followed me to the entrance to the big square and we spoke. It was easy to come to terms, though my conditions were tough. He doesn't ask about anything and his curiosity doesn't make him commit stupidities of any kind or drag me into problems that have nothing to do with me. He told me he was interested in storing a few crates of booze in my apartment. I agreed at first, then backed out. The neighborhood's very rough and the neighbors wouldn't stop talking if they discovered it. So I didn't get a discount on the usual price, just easier repayment terms. I had been without supplies for two whole months, a record period, and he offered to sell me some alcohol at the right time. We didn't speak again. He supplies me with what I need and I pay him depending on how much ready cash I have. The bookshop guy is incomprehensible, I mean inconsistent. He's smart and well informed but when it comes to the crunch he leaves all that aside and is a complete scammer. He treated me rudely the last time. He wouldn't give me any more time to pay, as he usually did. He made me repay all the money I owed and we started from scratch. I didn't ask him to show me his bookshop and I think he preferred I know nothing about him, other than that he sits in the café and talks big to his gang, as if he were lecturing at university or at a free thought forum. He uses his bookshop only as a front. Deception is common among all people, and the alcohol trade is very profitable, although the police do try to crack down on it. He works without a license and gets the beer from a factory on the road between the capital and Blida. Personally I don't care how much he makes from me. Money might not bring us happiness, but it can buy us oblivion.

I recently had a favor to ask of the bookshop man, the booze dealer. He was unexpectedly helpful. People with flexible principles can be very useful in hard times. He didn't help me for free, yet I'm grateful to him anyway. I'm a man who's grateful to an unhealthy extent, even toward those who don't really deserve it. The old man is ill and his memory's gone, I'm broke and helpless, and the old man's pension was stuck in the post office and mounting up. The postmaster is an old school friend of the bookshop man and maybe he sells him booze, just as he sells it to me. Ignoring the rules overcomes problems. The postmaster was well paid for ignoring them and on top of that he wanted me to thank him and show him gratitude that he didn't deserve. I didn't do it this time. As for the bookshop man, he was paid in full for his mediation, without having to sympathize with me as a regular customer who doesn't cause trouble, or with the old man who was his neighbor that I had got involved with. I gave them an appointment, after sunset, and they brought a large ledger with them. The postmaster checked that the old freedom fighter was still alive, then he stained the old man's index finger with ink and put his fingerprint on the ledger as proof that he had received his pension in full. I hardly spoke to the postmaster, beyond the usual greetings, and I just looked at the bookshop man with contempt because of his opportunism. They went off, leaving us with just a third of the money, and that third would have to take care of everything we needed for days, though there may not be that many days left. There was some furniture left that could be sold, but that could wait until the third ran out—the most important third in my life, and in his. I'm not prepared to work again and in practice that would be impossible. Who would look after the old man in my absence? I got him supplies of medicine and enough diapers to last until his early death, which I am looking forward to more than anything else. Inside me, that something bugs me whenever I think of leaving him alone and looking for somewhere else I can stay. I can't see the logic behind a messed-up insect like me having to face all these difficult ordeals. All the wretched insect wants to do is keep well out of the way, crawl under a rock or into a crack in the wall of an abandoned house, so that it isn't crushed under someone's foot.

What does it mean when your first romantic experiences are with a fat woman who looks like a lump of grease? That nurse had too much of everything except wisdom. I spoke to her obligingly but I was reluctant to go any further with her, on the grounds that I feared God and she had ruined all my dreams about women. When I later saw pictures of real women in sex magazines I found in the garbage, and compared them unfavorably with the nurse, I appreciated how much trouble I would have been in if, in my misery, I had given in to temptation and slept with her. Several times I almost abandoned my regime of chastity through reckless acts. I didn't ridicule her, because people should be judged by their character, but her large frame did impose its presence and there was no way to avoid it. Love is a winning card with women. She treated me better than anyone has ever treated me before. She bought me countless cigarettes and clothes, and she gave me special pills that make you feel as light as a feather floating in the air, happy with everything around you and prone to laugh at anything you see, even a funeral. That was the state I was in when I spoke to her about love and a life together and praised her figure and her elegance as if she were a Russian figure skater. I was her favorite in the hospital and I saw her colleagues making fun of her by winking at each other. I admit that the sight of us together was ridiculous. Once she came to me and complained about them, and I told her that jealousy can do worse things than that to women, and she shouldn't pay any attention to what they said. We agreed she would help me escape. I would disappear for days and then head to an apartment in Bachdjerrah for which she gave me the address. We would wait till the story was forgotten, then get married, and she would arrange everything. Her brother wouldn't object. He wanted to be spared the trouble of worrying about her, even if a mangy dog came and asked to marry her. In any case it's not my fault. The judicial system would forget me and we'd be happy, I told her. I played the role of the mangy dog and when I saw she was a little hesitant, hours before I regained my freedom, I barked a lot to assure her that I loved her and she had to wait for me. In the previous days we had avoided each other as much as possible so that she wouldn't be the first person suspected of helping me escape. Did they discover her role in my escape or is she still waiting for me?

One day I recklessly went out of the apartment to face the madness of the world around me with what was left of my sanity. I don't regret it at all; in fact, I consider it the best decision I ever made, at least as far as the first night is concerned. Luckily the water main came back on and I did a heroic job undoing the effects of the water shortage that the neighborhood had been through. I made my den look like a bridegroom's apartment on his wedding night. The night brings people countless blessings. The girl on the balcony and I had each made up our minds to take a step forward under cover of darkness, and in fact it was a massive leap for a man like me, a novice in such matters. The balcony light came on again and my excitement was well founded. Circumstances conspired to pave the way for a wonderful night. She's shy and not talkative. Maybe I had been unfair to her at first. She took the initiative to come and at the time I judged that she had a boldness that I didn't have. It was no use talking and I wasn't interested in that. I made do with the small lamp in my room. I welcomed her as one should, without pretending to be more generous than I could afford to be, because the fridge was empty. What good does talking do in such situations? The world of women is extraordinary. Does it make sense that I'd never been given a chance to explore it? Her silence made me anxious. It was an involuntary silence, or rather a laudable silence. Someone like her is the best person you could tell your secrets to or reveal your flaws to without fear that they might give you away. She was plump and agreeable, as fresh as she should be. She outdid me in daring and was bolder than me. I'm shy and I don't have a sense of humor. I left the lamp light low and I missed the chance to take a close look at her face. I might not recognize her if we met outside and in the street I wouldn't have the opportunity to check her identity by consulting my tactile memory of the contours of her body. We were hardly able to understand each other. The signals she gave were difficult to decipher and I'm not quick-witted. She was in a normal state at first but then she lost the power of speech for reasons I didn't understand. We agreed to repeat the first night and for the first time in my life I felt an emotion and attraction toward another human. I spent the day asleep and woke up in the afternoon, had a shave, and tried to get clean and neat, like a man that a woman might desire, even if she was mute. I went through periods when I thought that I was just hallucinating, that there was no light and no silhouette, or even a balcony in the first place. With certainty and strange enthusiasm, the old silhouettes won out. That bloody useless SIM card deserves to be cut up a thousand times. I had wasted all the money on the card speaking to that old German woman. I topped it up again, looked for that folded and scented piece of paper and the number written on it in pink ink, and dialed the number with considerable enthusiasm. Mubarak allowed me to put the SIM card in his phone. I made the call. She picked up, but I couldn't hear any response. I tried again twice within minutes, then gave the phone back to its owner and broke the SIM card. My experience on the first night was useful to me, and if I had to be grateful for anything in the world, it would be her body. How deprived I was! She was very short and she had hairy legs and yet I saw her as a real gift. I wished she had answered me and that we could have had a chat like two strangers who have long been ravaged by deprivation. She seemed like a good woman to me and I saw tears in her eyes when I told her about some of the things I had suffered. It was the first time I'd seen someone crying for my sake. She tried to explain many things to me but I didn't understand her. I didn't find out if she was living alone or not, or where she went to when she disappeared. I didn't even know her name.

Life went my way for a while, but then it stopped treating me nicely. One of the few things I gathered from her was that she had been inside the apartment in the past. That hurt me in a way I had never experienced before. I still have the luxury of feeling shocked, jealous, or angry about something against which I am powerless. The gullible pay double price every time. Mourad made his mark between her legs. She used to come to see him. She very much hated him. I didn't need to be a genius to work that out. And she isn't wholly nice. In fact she isn't nice at all. She went into the kitchen on her own, found the lighter easily, came back and lit a cigarette, and in bed she proved that there's a massive, an immeasurable difference between the amount of experience she has and the amount I have. She's a sex bitch. I was in an extremely bad mood. The darkness in the room hid my face, but I could see her smiling profusely. Maybe she wanted to give me an explanation, if she could get any words out. Who am I that she should give me an explanation? I'm used to allaying my hunger by devouring other people's leftovers. Their leftovers are not very appetizing, but I'm so hungry I'll eat anything. That same hunger drove me to have my way with her until the crack of dawn, although a pain I had never experienced before was still burning in my heart.

4

Vulgarity

I'VE BEEN STARING BLANKLY AT the wall for two hours like some useless old creature, as flaccid as the tits of an old bitch. It's not a pose that suits someone who has to act fast and wisely, but that's the way I am, and I have never claimed to be a man whose status has been misjudged by history. There is one question I've asked myself I don't know how many times: Who will walk in his funeral procession? It doesn't matter who walks in his funeral procession or what status they have. It would be best if no one saw him off and he walked alone to any cemetery in the neighborhood, determined not to come back and make me feel disgusted yet again. Good. I'm talking about him as if he really has gone to the other world and hasn't been snoring nearby throughout these two hours. I'm worried he might have fallen into a coma and I'll have to pursue my mission to the end, like a faithful dog that never leaves his master. The hospital is the best place for him, and I wouldn't want my intuition about his imminent demise to prove mistaken again, so let him go back there and recover, because my desire to dig his grave with my own hands knows no limits. The poor guy deserves a rest and I too deserve a chance to relax. I'm not even fit to look after myself and recently I've been gripped by a real fear of growing old. My life must stop soon and I must somehow disappear, but not before he passes away of course, otherwise I would no longer be a faithful dog. I worry about growing old and facing time alone in the last round. I've adapted to living alone permanently, but to die alone would be more than I could bear.

I've tried hard to make sure that the one third that the two thieves left us wouldn't run out or at least would last us as long as possible. My frugality has been admirable and I've been relatively successful. The old man lives at subsistence level so I've spent the greater part of it on myself. My love for life has been reactivated to some extent. I've spent five crazy nights like a newlywed. I bought perfume and fruit. I fed the old man well of course: it was his money. I was completely exhausted. It was hard work. Discovering the world of women isn't easy at all. She disappeared after that, as usual. There was no light from the balcony opposite and the shutters haven't been opened at night for her silhouette to tempt my lust. I felt as if I were fast asleep and I dreamed about a woman, then I woke up to find my pants wet. Even her features remained unclear, as if she had just flitted through my imagination and I hadn't really seen her. I was extremely cautious and nighttime also has its flaws. The margin for maneuver is very limited and death plays well in tight spaces. Yet I tried hard in a way. I asked the bookshop guy for help finding a male nurse and he was decent this time and didn't ask for anything in return for being humane. I brought a nurse to attach the tube to the dying man's arm. After he taught me how to adjust the rate of flow, all I had to do was change the bags of solution. I'm kinder than expected to him, but he won't have a chance to thank me for what I've done for him, even if he wants to.

In the morning I went out to the café and left him lying on the bed like a breathing corpse. It was one of the few times when I felt I wanted someone to help me. I found the café closed. I crossed the street, headed to another café, and ran into the imam. He ignored me when I greeted him. He continued on his way, so I followed him and asked him to visit the old man in order to help him recite the *shahada*, the profession of faith, before he dies. He hardly gave me a chance to speak. I started calling out to him as I followed him, but he shooed me away like a fly after asking me why I hadn't been praying in his mosque. I was about to tell him he could bring anyone he liked to the apartment without paying anything. All I was asking was for him to stay with me and advise me on what to do. I wanted him to recite some Quranic verses for the old man, because I only remember a few myself and I hadn't prayed since I stopped working for the pig. I didn't dare pick up a copy of the Quran. The five nights of fornication and the empty cans of beer in my apartment would need more than a token act of penitence. I had little sense of guilt and that was the major obstacle. Neither of us promised each other anything. I went to the mosque a little before the evening prayers, did my ablutions as a true worshipper should, and edged forward till I reached the front row. The imam saw me but didn't react. Just to prove my good intentions, as I did with the pig before, I wanted the imam to understand what I had done. A very reasonable price for saving the old man, whose soul was being tormented to no purpose. I was worried he was like me, lost and astray, and that he needed to hear the word of God, even from a man whose faith had been three-quarters compromised by contact with that woman's blue nightshirt.

I came back unsuccessful and then another night descended on me, with the old man waking up every two or three hours. I gave him some water to drink. He opened his eyes with difficulty, then sank back into a distant world. His breathing was heavy and he sounded like someone climbing a mountain with a heavy weight. Life is like a deep pit and it requires unusual effort to climb out of it. I forgot the question about who would attend his funeral and despised myself. I'm pathetic and really unbalanced and this breathing corpse deserves to be thanked. He has restored my humanity and God has given me another father, albeit in the form of a man about to die. A more vital question has been troubling me since sunset: Who will dig the grave? I don't know where the cemetery is or whether he has any relatives who can dig his grave. He doesn't have anyone asking after him. It's a tragedy when someone dies without anyone noticing his passing, like an animal that dies in the wilderness. I'm going to have many more problems with him after he dies than I have while he's alive. He'll have to be carried to the hospital as a lifeless corpse, a medical certificate will have to be issued to say that he died of natural causes, and then the procurator has to approve a death certificate. Then there's the burial permit from the municipality and I don't know what. With all that to do, I would be visible like everyone else, unable to keep out of sight of anything, and the boundaries between me and the world would dissolve, leaving me exposed. That's unthinkable. If he dies, I'll arrange for him to be buried immediately in the cemetery or some other piece of ground, somewhere unlikely to be discovered. That's a challenge that goes way beyond any compassion I might have toward the poor old man or loyalty to his son, an almost-friend who emigrated and left no tracks.

I woke up at dawn, checked him and found he hadn't died. I won't say "unfortunately" because there are many challenges. It wasn't long before someone knocked on the door. It was the imam, sporting a white cloak like an angel judging the goodness of our intentions and fulfilling his implicit promises. He sat by the old man's head. His eyes half open, he solemnly recited the Quran. He recited many verses. He recited and sometimes looked at me, and for some reason I imagined that he wanted the old man to die. The apartment might be vacant then and he could make a very profitable deal with me, and later I would train under him—exorcizing djinn isn't a trade that's impossible to learn. I would dress up in white and become an angel like him and embrace the life I was escaping from. He finished his recitation and asked for some water. I brought him a bottle of mineral water. He recited over it, muttering at length, and then told me to give the old man some of it to drink. The old man's eyes glazed over again and he went off into his own world. The angel left after that, leaving the devil that was me living his ordeal. Another tedious day and I'm pretty much like a frog that has just reached menopause. Time is passing and it makes no sense to linger any longer. It occurred to me to take the old man and throw him in an old people's home. They would know how to look after him there. I hurried out and spoke to the bookshop man who sells oblivion. I put the suggestion to him enthusiastically but he dashed almost all my expectations. It's difficult, was the frustrating conclusion of his thoughts on the subject. Nonetheless, I thought it might be possible. Bribes open every door and his condition doesn't offer grounds for hope. He wouldn't stay long in the old people's home and he wouldn't feel anything. He'd probably die within a few days. That's if death is gracious and comes a little late.

All my dark emotions took a back seat and I felt very sorry for him. He really was a poor guy. His voice was very weak and I could see him rolling his heavy eyes. He had stopped calling for Mourad. His life was slipping away and his death was close. This was a decisive night. Would he hold out till the morning? What a lot of questions I had. Kada al-Bayaa, the police informer, had started watching me. He hadn't done that since that time when he followed me to the station, hung around in the square, and pretended he was waiting for someone. He has the senses of a police dog. I asked the bookshop man if I could depend on him. He didn't give me any specific advice, but said, Be careful. The poor old man won't have a funeral and no one will hear he has died. He disappeared from sight years ago and his passing won't pique the curiosity of those who had forgotten him even when he was alive. Only a man without principles is fit for a task like this, I said, as I encouraged myself to go ahead with the plan I had devised. Looking out of the kitchen window, I saw Kada and asked him what he was looking for, but he didn't answer. I gestured to him and he came over to my place. A real dog, he is. This man you can see is dying, I said, pointing at the old man, and he needs a grave. His son is abroad and has abandoned him and I can't handle it for reasons from the past. The legal procedures require documents and I don't have an ID card, and I don't want to be anyone at all. He listened to me in silence and lingered as he worked out how much he could charge for doing me a favor. I told him about the idea of putting the poor man in an old people's home, although it's almost too late. We should let him die in peace, he said cunningly, and then I left him to think. The cemetery guard is his friend. That was good news for me. We would just have to make sure no one asks any questions about the dead man. He thought of him as dead and went on talking. The fear is that Mourad or one of his relatives might come back and ask about the grave and who buried him. Mourad will never come back and the dead man doesn't have any other relatives, I assured him confidently. He smiled. I waited to hear how much money he would want in return, but he didn't ask for anything. The burial would take place at night and we would go in through the back gate of the cemetery. You'll be with us, he said. I agreed in principle. Won't we say some prayers at the grave side? I asked him. The cemetery guard is addicted to various psychotropic pills but he does pray sometimes, he said, trying to reassure me. Damn! His coldness annoyed me. He sounded like a criminal who had killed people and committed other heinous acts. I wanted to throw him out immediately. The alternative was to disappear and leave the old man to his fate until he died, and then the smell of his body would take care of the rest.

Did I look to Kada like someone who has a fortune? The bastard asked me for a very large sum of money. The old man has plenty of money in the bank, he said in a cunning tone, and it wasn't fair that it should all go to me. I didn't tell him we were almost broke. I left some space for greed to keep him interested. It occurred to me that I might really seem to him like someone who has a treasure or massive wealth and that's why he would cooperate with me. We agreed he would take care of everything, with me at a distance. They would dig the grave, buy the shroud, and wash him. That's my job, he assured me. Then he asked me when I would pay him. Logically I should have replied, I'll pay when the man dies, but I wanted to leave the door ajar again, so I said, Don't worry, very soon. I saw he was lukewarm about it. Something had dampened his initial enthusiasm. Perhaps he thought the job wouldn't materialize. He'd lived in the neighborhood for many years and maybe he knew that the old man had come close to death several times and then hadn't died, and if he didn't die there wouldn't be a job and he wouldn't make any money. I was terrified of that: he might take advantage of my absence and kill him, so that then I would have to deal with his death, and then I would inevitably ask him for help and would be asked to pay a large amount that I didn't have. For some reason I made a slip of the tongue: I'm going to receive a quantity of gold and I'll pay you whatever you want, I said with feigned confidence. His eyes lit up. A large quantity? Yes, the deal isn't quite done but I'll do it soon. After that we spoke for some minutes, then he went off, showing complete sympathy for the sick old man and assuming I would believe him. I rather regretted it. He might kill me when it occurs to him that I promised him an illusion or he might denounce me to the police. I heard the old man snoring loudly. Then the snoring stopped so I ran back to his room, but luckily he hadn't died yet.

No doubt the crow that dug the first grave in history would have laughed at me. What's the problem? You can dig a grave anywhere and have done with it. Giving advice to others is easy and that same crow probably ended up lying dead in the sun at the mercy of the worms, with no other crow to bury it. After midnight facts seem clearer. Who can give me an assurance that, when he discovers that I've lied, Kada won't denounce me to the person who employs him and then get paid for it? Who cares about an insect like me? Who would pay even one dinar to find out which shithole I was hiding in? It was a stupid move on my part to tempt him, very stupid. I warned him not to try monitoring my activities again and explained that if he visited me too often it might attract the neighbors' attention. Even so, he came back looking cocky and everything about him told me he was a mean bastard. He asked me to let him stay the night in the apartment. That was total blackmail and in fact it was the first price I paid for my foolish move. He disappeared and came back half an hour later, accompanied by the cemetery guard who would supposedly be our partner in the plan to sort out my whole predicament. He also brought a woman, who turned out to be none other than the woman in the blue nightshirt, the woman that the imam falsely claimed was his second wife. She isn't just his. The local men also have shares in her and I don't rule out the possibility that the bookshop man and Mubarak are among them. She's employed by an old woman who looks like a devil and behaves like one, I expect. The woman brought her to the entrance of the building as she did the first time. She waited a while and then left. I didn't need to spy on them and I didn't even wonder what a cemetery guard was doing with a woman who was a common prostitute. It's the apartment's fate to be a den of iniquity and there's nothing I can do to stop it.

Kada didn't stop watching me. He looked at me suspiciously and I felt I was in his power. For the first time in my life I wished I was a killer. Some scores can only be settled by murder. I closed the door on the old man firmly and went out to the café. This time I found it open. The inquisitive gang were all there and in the middle was Mubarak, who had come back from being away and avoided looking at me. Maybe he regretted being too hasty. He shouldn't have told me anything about his plan before checking I was fully prepared to take part. Who said I wasn't prepared? I was worried he might have gone ahead without me and then come back. He look sullen and, when our eyes met, I read in his eyes a message that seemed to say, What a coward you are! As if I had ever claimed to be brave in his presence. Kada winked at me, suggesting we shared some big secret. I don't rule out him being gay. A mere dog. I got involved with him and the miscalculations between us had piled up. Finally he left and I was worried he might take advantage of my absence and go and kill the old man. I followed him to the door and saw him head in the other direction. I went back to my seat in the café. I've started avoiding the apartment. Minutes passed and Mubarak sat down with me. Casually he asked me when I would settle my account with him. Very soon, I replied nonchalantly. The bill had mounted up for a month or more, I don't remember. I showed him I was displeased and saw it as an inauspicious start. He wanted to put pressure on me to agree. I'm willing, I said, but he didn't reply. Then he went off to his group. We waited many minutes till the inquisitive group left. I pretended I was engrossed in a newspaper and unaware of what was happening. The way they looked at me gave them away, but what I discovered was really interesting. None of them had told any of the others that they had had dealings with me. Mubarak and I whispered to each other. He had gone away in recent days to inspect the abandoned cemetery in the place he again refused to name before the time came, although he was sure that no one knew his big secret. I told him I couldn't leave the old man alone and we agreed to find someone to look after him during my absence. He insisted I pay the person who looked after the old man, as well as the taxi fare to the town closest to the cemetery. I agreed and didn't dare say I was broke. I was so worried about Kada that I agreed. I had done without beer for a while and, before leaving, the bookshop man looked at me as if I had broken a sacred agreement with him. Money doesn't interest me in the least and my memories of the mute woman with the hairy legs have almost disappeared, just as her voice disappeared earlier. I was worried Kada might seek revenge on me. He's willing to kill despite his docile appearance. The boundaries between me and the rest of the world were going to collapse—in fact, they had collapsed. I realized that when I found it hard to leave the café and go back to the apartment. I was serious about the adventure with Mubarak. I wanted to pay Kada, bury the old man, and have done with it.

Does an unsuccessful crow such as me have to pay the price for failing to hide its flaws? I stood by the café door and wondered where to go after arranging the old man's burial, and if I had to leave, what would force me to pay the money? I could leave the old man and make a new life for myself with the gold. No one has ever died and gone without a grave forever. I was very confused and the pangs of that something inside me were very intense and severe. Several times in the past I had been about to abandon him, but those pangs were an effective deterrent. They made a deep impression inside me. I was sure that Kada was lying in wait for me. He took me by surprise, standing at the door with Mubarak. He wanted to know who I was dealing with, and he'd already searched the apartment. He was looking for clues that would help him track down the alleged gold.

I came back from the café and found the old man in a critical condition. He wasn't going to hold out much longer and could soon be considered dead. It isn't hard to face an obvious fact like death when you're a man who's lived in the shadows in some sense, and who has never wanted to look like one of those he saw among the living. Even so, my options were limited and I had to decide. Should I honor the dead man by burying him, or should I save myself? I imagined I'd heard him breathing a little earlier, but in fact his eyes had glazed over, his mouth was open, and that was it. I couldn't guess what he felt when his time came. I had turned up a little late, and the situation left me rather colder than I had expected. I remembered how cold I was when my garbage collector friend was crushed to death under the wheel of the garbage truck. In this case the death was commonplace, the most likely outcome. I had wanted to give him a gentle death. My heart had recovered its kindness, or almost. I imagine he wanted to prove to me that he would have the last word and that, despite his weakness, he could make such an important decision without me. Maybe I should go with him and see what it's like to be dead. Why hadn't I thought before about trying out death, if only once? He was completely still and his body had started to go cold. I preferred to leave him alone for a while. It was his right to sink into the moment without anyone disturbing him, since death is more intimate than life. He passed away after using up all his diapers and all he left me was his body and the last bag of rice that we had. Rare generosity. I'm the sole heir of a dead man who's lying desti-tute, without even a sad tear for his sake. I expect the angels made sure he recited the *shahada*, if they weren't too busy with someone more important who was also dying. He's as unlucky as me and everyone beats him to everything. My conscience is senile and its fangs have fallen out. He kept watching me as I packed my bag, the same backpack I brought with me when I first came, but without the books or the laptop. I felt I was betraying someone, though I didn't know exactly who and I didn't care. He wasn't my father in any case and the emotions I tricked myself into feeling in order to bear with him died when he died. I admit I'm a failed crow and I'm right not to commit myself to any promise that I can't fulfill. I'll just become a dog. I've paid the instalments to Mourad in full and also to my notional father. This night is a landmark night and it deserves a special celebration if that devil of a bookshop guy will agree to sell me some booze on account. I'll celebrate the fact that yet again I'm just a dog and I've been relieved of a burden. On my way back from the café I saw a police car in the neighborhood. It definitely didn't come for fun, so now it's time for me to leave this place. I'd kill myself before they could get their hands on me. When you go mad nothing is taboo. I packed my bag minutes ago. I have no destination but I'll wait till it's pitch black and then leave. I'm thinking of finding Mubarak and encouraging him to prove with his gold that my luck isn't always bad. All I have to do is leave the apartment door half open so that the neighbors will find out tomorrow that the old man is just a rotting corpse. Then I'll go back where I came from. I may go back to Serdj El Ghoul, because I miss my brother Ammar, and visit the forest of death where life called me back from the brink and postponed the moment of death. I'm thinking of going back to work as a garbage collector, if I'm given the chance. I spent the happiest days of my life amidst the garbage. I admit I was just a piece of rubbish living in its rightful place. But I'm incapable of making any decision. I served this corpse gallantly, but unfortunately he won't be able to repay the favor by giving me any advice, however trivial it might be. I miss my aunt. She also died and left me. Her presence stood between me and all the doors of hell. I've been remiss about visiting the graves of those who gave me boundless love and who had to die because of that. I really do have in mind to go back where I came from. The remnants of the good sense I escaped with, in order to face the madness of the world around me, have now run out and no spoils are worth the effort any longer. In the courtyard outside that mental hospital I'll tell them I'm sorry and they'll know how to make me dopey and embalmed, so that I'm always happy. I'd have to renounce the idea that life is worth escaping to. It was a seductive adventure and yet I had to be that mad in order to plunge back into life. I jumped off the high wall, almost broke my foot, and went through hell to save myself from those devils wearing bright white coats and to win my name back. I completely failed to do that, but now I long for them and I want to embrace them one by one. I'm driven by a desire to ask them to help me disappear again, so that I'm no one at all, not even me. Who am I?

That fat nurse is the only person I've wronged in my life and she deserves a long apology because I tricked her in the name of love for the sake of an illusory escape.

I took several steps to the kitchen window. The darkness had descended but I spotted Kada standing behind a large tree in the middle of the square, playing with his phone, and pretending as usual that he was waiting for someone. I went back to the dead man, looked at his dead face, and realized that any joy we had experienced, or any happiness that had ever filled our hearts, would be meaningless if this was how we ended. My fear that the bastard might jump out on me in the dark was unjustified as long as he hadn't found out where the gold was. Even so, my heart started to pound. More minutes passed. I had calmed down completely. When I heard someone knocking on the door, I went to open it without a care in the world, and I saw him through the peep hole.

Hell Looks Out of the Window

5

Ingenuous Preliminaries

RAFIK NASSIRI'S LONGSTANDING FASCINATION WITH his own career as a brilliant detective ebbed away as he grumpily climbed the stairs to the top floor, heading to the office of the police commissioner. Under his arm he carried a file of inconsequential documents. You're judged by results and in this case the mission was to track down the wanted man. But Rafik—and he alone—had come back empty-handed. This was the third time in ten days he had been summoned to say what progress he had made in the case. Now he had started to have doubts even about the wanted man's name and, as he knocked on the door, he began to wonder if the man ever existed in the first place. Was his boss playing games with him? And why might they be targeting him? He had been obedient and hardworking for twenty years, he was as sharp as a trained dog, and he had no enemies worth mentioning, just people with whom he might have had passing disagreements.

The commissioner returned his greeting. "I hope you've found him, or at least found out where he's gone," he added. "We have to tell them something. In the end we're not looking for a ghost," he continued, but he sounded like he expected a disappointing response.

Rafik didn't utter a word. He didn't intend to apologize profusely to justify his failure. The commissioner, Abdel Ouahab Chaal, waited for him to say something but was then distracted by a phone call, which alleviated the awkwardness for the minutes he was talking. Then he went back to looking at the detective.

"Sir, I found myself in an unprecedented situation and I'm sorry to say the man couldn't be found," said Rafik.

After an unexpected calm, the commissioner grew agitated again. He lit a cigarette and blew the smoke out slowly and methodically, like someone in the habit of setting the tempo for everything. The detective repeated what he had said in another way, this time with the insistence of someone who wants to emphasize the exceptional nature of the situation.

"There's no trace of him, sir. Or, to be more precise, he's a man whose tracks have been completely obliterated. He might exist, but he's no one," he said. "What else can I say?" he continued after a quick pause. "He might have existed but in effect he doesn't exist now."

The commissioner angrily dismissed what he had heard. He was a man accustomed to obedience and tangible results, a man who hated inconsistencies and riddles that couldn't be solved. "Might he have died?" he said in bewilderment. "Might he have been kidnapped? Killed himself and his body decomposed like a dog that's died without anyone noticing? What's his story and where did this 'no one' disappear to?"

The detective started to go into detail, avoiding looking directly into the commissioner's eyes. In the neighborhood where the wanted man was supposed to be living, the residents had given contradictory statements. They knew him and they didn't know him. They gave irreconcilable accounts of his name and his appearance. Everyone knew him and no one knew him. He was an introvert who avoided everyone and sometimes wasn't seen for weeks. The lights at his apartment had been on but there was no noise inside. The owner, the dead man, had been elderly and infirm, and he had one son who had emigrated to Germany. It was the son who had rented the apartment without a contract.

"When we inspected the apartment, it was clean and tidy. There were some food leftovers on a small table, a bag of rice, a lighter, an ashtray, and some other insignificant things dispersed around the bedroom, including an empty perfume bottle. The other rooms were completely unfurnished and closed up. The strange thing is that we didn't find any fingerprints, as if the person living there had had their fingers cut off. I went to ask a shopkeeper nearby, and then the owner of a nearby café, and they both said they had seen him a few times, but the puzzling thing was that they were speaking about different people."

The detective stopped and looked deep into the commissioner's eyes to find out if he should continue. The man gave him no sign, so he continued: "The problem is we don't have a recent picture of him, just an old one from when he was a teenager and a very worn-out copy from an ID card that expired eight years ago, and the file for that in the archives went missing when the municipality where he was registered was moving to its new headquarters. Commissioner, sir, I've often wondered if he goes around in disguise sometimes because, according to those who've described him, he once appeared as a man in his seventies with gray hair and wearing thick glasses, and limping slightly, and another time as a man in his forties, healthy but with a haggard face, like someone with a long history of misfortune. And when we asked other government departments whether he appeared on their lists of suspects they said he didn't. There's no passport in his name and the border police say no one by that name has left the country or entered the country in the last ten years. In the Interior Ministry they told us there are dozens of people with the same name and with similar particulars."

"Ah, his particulars?"

"That's just about it, sir."

"That's nothing, comrade. You lot have been playing around."

"There's no name in the courts, nor in the lists of missing people. There's no trace of him in the hospitals, or even in the death certificates or burial permits."

He stopped a while, got his breath back and looked up at the commissioner.

"You might make fun of me if I told you how much trouble this guy gave me making inquiries after him," Rafik added.

"What?"

The detective wiped his forehead and, despite his embarrassment, told the commissioner he had gone to the imam of the Takoua mosque in the neighborhood and asked about the man. The imam hadn't told him anything definite, so he had asked if the djinn ever kidnap people. Abdel Ouahab Chaal let out a prolonged laugh and slammed his fist down on his desk. "Stop. I'm not in the mood to laugh. Has some devil possessed him and flown off with his body? Has he been roaming around the streets and towns like a dervish? Who is he and where is he?"

The detective asked to take his leave, said goodbye, and left. But first he asked to be relieved of his assignment to track down this particular man. Detectives hate reaching a dead end. Their job is to solve mysteries and he had failed. He insisted on his request even after he was warned it might damage his stellar career as a detective. He went down the stairs, and at the gate he stopped and carefully examined all the people walking past him. In each of them he saw something of this Nobody that they had described to him and that he hadn't been able to find. Each of them had something of him and this Nobody could be a part of all those he saw walking past, as if he had melted into the multitude.

The commissioner had known Rafik a long time. The detective clearly didn't have enough enthusiasm to bring about a breakthrough in the case, so he decided to give him a break for a while, in the hope that he'd do better when he came back. The detective had started losing enthusiasm for his work anyway, after receiving threats in connection with a real estate corruption case. The investigation into that case had been suspended and finally abandoned. The country was riddled with corruption and that was no secret. Although the detective knew about the corruption, he did feel he had been stabbed in the back and that he was now without protection. The heart isn't a machine that never tires and he had lived through many similar cases, even if they hadn't reached the stage of him being physically threatened. But this time he'd had his fill. He'd told the commissioner he had decided to put in a request for early retirement, or even to submit his resignation and, if that was rejected, to neglect his job so seriously that he would be dismissed for abandoning his duty. Running away is the strategy chosen by cowards. No one had ever accused him of that, although people were now so demoralized that there was no longer any point in fighting for anything. Life is difficult and being forced to obey is painful and sometimes humiliating. He understood all that and he was well aware that doing one's duty has its limits for someone who wants to retain his dignity. Colleagues from the same intake as him had grown rich from the job. They had come to terms with the decadence, and when they found it was impossible to prevent evildoing, they thought it would be stupid not to take advantage of it. He had continued to swim against the tide. But everything has its limits. The obligation to do one's duty comes to an end when the rule of law starts to break down. To deter the big chiefs it takes more than one enthusiastic officer or an honest judge who knows the penal code by heart.

He liked to take on the challenge of solving big puzzles. That's why the commissioner had banked on him and been unusually patient with him. He thought about the case for two days and couldn't make up his mind. It was a simple case but puzzling, and it might not deserve any special attention. First impressions are dangerous and a detective can become trapped or misled by them. Something was making him uneasy. What did it mean when he couldn't find any lead to track down a man who had lived in a rough neighborhood and then disappeared without a trace, when the most he had managed to glean, after going back and forth, was a few contradictory statements? He reckoned he must be dealing with an extraordinary man who had tricked everyone. Who had killed the old man? And was he really murdered? The forensic pathologist said that Suleiman Bennaoui, eighty-seven years old, had probably died of a heart attack four days before he was found. In his report he wrote that there were no signs of violence on the body. Rafik had learned from previous experiences not to take the word of a forensic pathologist as indisputable, so he took the report simply as one element that might give one hypothesis more weight than another.

On a cloudy Thursday morning in January, an informer told the police that an old man had died in his apartment on the top floor of the fourth building to the right from the entrance to the One Hundred Houses area near the railway station in Rouïba. The putrid smell had caught the attention of the neighbors and the front door of the apartment was unlocked, so they went in and saw that their neighbor's dead body had turned dark blue and started to decompose. The dead man was found lying on a long sofa. The television in front of him was broadcasting a recitation from the Quran and a tube attached to an empty bag of solution was still inserted in his arm. The deceased, Suleiman Bennaoui, was from Bordj Menaïel and had fought in the War of Independence. He had one son called Mourad and no one knew why he had left him and gone off. Mourad had been living in the apartment next door to his father's, probably renting it cheaply from the owner, a man who worked for a company in the south and had had many problems with the neighbors. He had brought women to the apartment and on one occasion the women and children ganged up on him and besieged him until the police came. He left in disgrace and never went back. Mourad got engaged to one of his relatives and a week before they were due to be married, he broke off the engagement, and disappeared three months later. No one had seen him since.

Suleiman Bennaoui continued to pray in the mosque until about a year ago, when he was incapacitated by disease and stayed at home. He was friendly with everyone and was not known to have any enemies or to have done anything that might make anyone seek revenge in any way. There was nothing suspicious about the state of the apartment. His papers were untouched and the crime certainly had nothing to do with theft, although no money was found at the scene. Rafik had not decided whether the old man's death resulted from a crime and his main interest was to find the young man who had lived with him for the last months of his life. Someone said this young man had last been seen a week earlier, that is three days before the death, while the café owner there, who was known as Uncle Mubarak, said he had been away in the days before the old man's death and did not know anything. The informer assigned to the station district, who was meant to be the government's eyes and ears but in this case was struck blind, had nothing to say. He was apparently unaware of what was going on around him. When Rafik saw Suleiman Bennaoui's body, he had the impression the man had been lucky to live as long as he had. He was emaciated, his cheekbones protruded, and he should probably have died several times over already. In the living room, where he was found, there was a photograph of him on the wall, in military uniform with a gun, standing next to some other people. Another picture on the wall opposite showed him with bushy eyebrows and a full, healthy face. A manly mustache was his most distinctive feature.

The neighbors said that the young man who looked after him was a friend of Mourad's, or a relative of theirs who had come from far away. Others said that the old man lived on his own and they hadn't seen anyone go into or come out of his apartment. The woman who used to clean for them had moved from her shanty home a while ago. Her husband had died in a small metalwork factory and, since he had no insurance, she received no compensation. She adapted to her new circumstances by working in the home of Uncle Suleiman, as she called him. Rafik found out her name was Saadia by consulting the local authority's lists of rehoused people, and he asked her about the young man and if he might have killed Suleiman. Saadia said that it was inconceivable and that he was a nice person. He used to complain about looking after him, but he never abandoned him. He had taken him to the hospital when his condition deteriorated. She paused a while and seemed to be really sad about the old man. Then she said the young man was like God's gift to Suleiman. He looked after the old man as a son should look after his father, or even better. The poor old man was ill and had been expected to die any day. Asked about the young man's name, she said Suleiman used to call him Mourad but she didn't always see him and she exchanged words with him only a few times. Saadia struck him as honest and extremely objective, although she didn't hide her sympathy for the mysterious young man. She was too young to be a mother to him. Everything was possible, and she would definitely recognize him easily if she saw him again or if she saw a picture of him. Saadia had looked after everything in the old man's house and what she said about having only a few meetings with him was not entirely truthful. She wanted to avoid being dragged into a complicated criminal investigation. Rafik had assumed that the mysterious man was Mourad himself and that he had run away out of shock at his father's death or for some other reason. But he ruled out that assumption when he heard her account of events, and when the border police later confirmed that the man called Mourad Bennaoui was abroad.

Mourad's name appeared on the list of travelers leaving the country and Rafik looked in vain for a way to tell him that his father had died. He had left for Germany a year earlier, abandoning his father right at the end of his life—behavior that might look quite deplorable to someone who has the time and leisure to feel surprised at everything new that humans come up with. With maternal compassion, the government took care of burying the old man. The neighbors gathered around in shock and children were kept away from the scene while the *Protection Civile* people moved the decomposing corpse to the hospital. A correspondent from one of the TV channels was there, looking for a scoop. He seemed eager, but with his modest experience he was unable to obtain a single important statement. In the evening some viewers gave the news minimal attention when it appeared on a streamer at the bottom of the screen during an advert for Always sanitary pads. The forensic pathologist had had a sleepless night—too much attention to detail is a strain on the heart, and no report he had written had ever brought anyone back to life, so the gains to be expected from his examination of the body were very limited. The report went to some department and was then buried in the archives, just as the person it was written about would be buried. In the morning the body was brought back to the neighborhood in a coffin. In the hospital they washed and shrouded the corpse at government expense. At the funeral in the Takoua mosque, Cheikh Hassan Daffaf said prayers for him with a heart that was only half reverent. He was grateful for the death because it eliminated a possible witness, may God protect humankind. As the coffin lay in front of him, a blue haze clouded his vision, and in his heart he felt a mixture of nostalgia and desire. He tried but failed to internalize an insincere sense of repentance. Time can solve anything and a clean record requires that no flaws are visible. Where had that man gone, the one whose name he didn't know? He hoped he would disappear forever, that he would vanish into thin air and remain a phantasm, as he had been to him when he met him. A clean record that would clear the way to glory for him. He was not the kind of person who sought worldly advantage at the expense of his religion, but it is virtuous to strive for high office. He had been nominated for the position of dean of the city's imams and he was going to move to the city's biggest mosque. The old dean had died and Cheikh Hassan was the man best placed to succeed him. The security agencies had recommended him and were grateful for his cooperation, and his path seemed to be clear. Some well-meaning neighbors had asked an itinerant merchant from Bordj Menaïel to tell the old man's relatives of his death, if he still had any family left in his hometown. It was a futile effort. The old man had lived far away and no one remembered him. Twenty men or less took part in the funeral procession. Two of them had volunteered to dig the grave and they were helped by two workers from the municipality. Since he had fought in the War of Independence, he deserved to be spared any further humiliation and his body should not remain a source of permanent revulsion. It wasn't a happy ending in any case. Dying alone, with no one to shed a tear of sadness, is not something he could boast about to the heavenly hosts. But he finally found a grave, and the old saying proved true: "No one remains without a grave forever."

The cemetery was guarded by Djelal, a man who managed to live on only one quarter of his senses. Life is crazy and cannot bear too much awareness. The guard had in fact visited Mourad's apartment not so long ago. Silence is a strong shield, the government is inquisitive by nature and might continue to investigate, and everyone would rather do without being questioned. From early childhood he had heard people call him Bleary Eyes. But his birth certificate gave another name, one he felt had nothing to do with him. People aren't even free to choose the names they like, he once said to his only friend, Kada, the police informer who was known to everyone living in the station district. As if his name was the most serious problem he faced in life. He lived his life ignored, in a hut in the cemetery, where he worked and lived permanently, in perfect harmony with the dead. Sometimes he visited his mother and brothers, spent generously on them, and then came back to play dominoes with young men till late at night. His work gave him a chance to take symbolic revenge. Not far from the cemetery there were rich people living in villas. They went out in their cars every morning to make more money and came home late at night after spending the evenings with their mistresses, telling them that money doesn't bring happiness. Their well-groomed daughters headed to school and their scowling wives went on spending sprees to forget how tedious and unpleasant it was to live in the company of their unfaithful husbands. And he just sat at the cemetery gate seeing how their lives progressed smoothly while for him time was frozen and he waited to join those lying at rest inside the cemetery. Only when they died was he allowed to be master over them. The ground swallowed them up, everyone forgot them, and then they were at his mercy. When he was half-conscious, he could do deals if he wanted and make money from the remains of their bodies, which had themselves thrived on ill-gotten gains. The biggest cemetery in Rouïba, where there are factories and villas, was the scene for another act of revenge—the grave-robbing that he carried out, unknown to anyone else. He had no score to settle with the people buried and no reason to seek revenge, whatever their rank in life might have been. He felt a little sad for them. He knew from the number of mourners what kind of lives they had led, and what status they had among the mourners.

Some of the local people—the café owner and a group of his friends, including Cheikh Hassan Daffaf—misled the investigation, either deliberately or not, in that they gave conflicting testimony and smiled inanely, and the damned informer assigned to the neighborhood didn't tell the detective anything. In their statements they each gave Rafik reason to believe that someone else among them might be the missing man, and it looked like they were making fun of him. A detective doesn't have to believe everything he's told, and he saw this as merely an incidental distraction, but in the end he came up with almost nothing anyway. The mystery man had been there but there was no trace he'd been there. Was it conceivable that they didn't even know the man's name? Or that they couldn't agree on what he looked like or that they gave ridiculously varying estimates of his age? He went back and lay on his bed till nighttime. In the morning he had to brief the commissioner on the latest developments, but what developments were there? There was no solid information. He opened the window and a cold breeze blew in. He thought he should stop deceiving himself. This endless pursuit of new secrets to uncover and being up to his ears in work. For what? He didn't have anyone waiting for him in the evening and he spent every weekend as insubstantial as the wind, as hollow as a reed. He worked himself to death in order to forget he was alone and deprived in a way that might be unprecedented. Now he had a chance to rest. He hadn't taken his annual vacation for three years, but now he should. That was the conversation he had with himself every night. He thought over his life at length, then went to sleep, woke up early in the morning, and headed off to work as if all the advice he had given himself was just hot air. Hoda was waiting for him but he was reluctant to accept that she was his future, as if he were being dragged to his death. He closed the window, had a short nap, and then went back to thinking. His sympathy for the old man was straightforward and superficial: what had caught his interest was the young man who had lived with the old man until his death. It wasn't exactly solving a hypothetical crime that preoccupied him. It was where the young man had come from, where he had gone, and how everyone had come to see him as no one.

6

Someone is Hiding a Secret

"Shouldn't we first ask where that man came from, and then it would be easier to find out how he disappeared later?" said Ousmane La Gauche, calmly and confidently, glancing around at the people who had been seated for the past hour at the same table in the middle of Mubarak's café. No one challenged the soundness of the question. The man had a sharp tongue, his vocabulary was vast, and he had a long history of being argumentative. He had been hot-tempered recently for reasons that he didn't disclose. He had gone to university after passing his baccalaureate at the age of thirty, but he gave up after two years because he came to see university graduates as a bunch of ignoramuses and argued that philosophy should be a way of life, not a subject that's taught and examined. He turned to politics and thought he had leadership qualities that should be given a chance to flourish. In the end he succumbed to reality, opened a bookshop, and lived off the earnings from that.

"I'm not interested in him in any way. He can go to hell," said Mubarak, as if he were revealing a secret. "What really matters to me is the last month's bill he didn't pay. Cunning bastard. He left the day before he was due to pay." Silence reigned again. The session ended. They had said everything that could be said, and that afternoon they had to decide what to do about him: should they tell the authorities what they knew, or should they ignore him, as if he were a dog that had gone missing or died somewhere unknown? He had disappeared a week earlier and no one had seen a sign of him since. Okay, maybe he had gone travelling or changed his place of residence. He didn't need to ask anyone for permission to do that. He wasn't a friend to any of them. In fact none of them had ever sat with him or tried to get acquainted. With them it hadn't gone beyond saying hello and smiling politely.

There was little noise in the half-empty café. Mubarak was a miserly man. He hadn't kept up with the modern cafés and tea salons by replacing the windows, renovating the décor, or furnishing the place properly. It was just a forgotten café in a forgotten suburb. It takes all sorts to make a world. Cheikh Hassan Daffaf stroked his beard and said, "As it says in the Quran, 'And do not pursue that of which you have no knowledge.' Even so, and with good intentions, I sent someone around to the imams of all the mosques in the city and gave them a description of this man, as I heard it from you yesterday. None of them think they have seen him." He paused a moment, and then said resignedly: "I think we should leave him to God. I've never seen him praying behind me in our local mosque, and all I can do is pray that God will guide him and have mercy on him, if the man has indeed gone to meet his Maker." The sheikh then walked off without waiting to see their reaction to what he had said. Ousmane La Gauche didn't have a chance to challenge him, but when he was gone he said it was a mistake to ask "that bigot" for help and that the sheikh thought God was his private property, his own Lord and not anyone else's. "Now we're spared his scowling face," he said. "These people think it's beneath them to sit in a café like this and mix with ordinary people."

"The man had been sitting at the same table close to the window for a whole year," said the informer. "It was reserved for him. He came in, looking down at the floor, oblivious to everyone, with a folded newspaper under his arm, and always dressed the same way—faded blue jeans and a black jacket, with a small beard that never seemed to grow, and some remnants of hair on the top of his head that suggested that the nickname Baldy would suit him well. I was stupid. How could a sleuth underestimate such a person? All I can hope for is that the old man's tragic death has nothing to do with his disappearance. Am I worried I might be accused of negligence?" Bored, his audience listened to what the man repeatedly said. Kada the Informer, which is what they called him in his absence, was an old resident of the neighborhood. He had been on the rebel side in the civil war, but then he had seen the error of his ways and took advantage of the amnesty law. Then he went to the other extreme, wholly loyal to the security agencies, and rose to the rank of "informer." "One morning, a morning like any other meaningless morning, I saw him. Then he disappeared without a trace. I used to call him Mr. Doesn't Care. Once I followed him and I think he noticed. He didn't turn to look at me and he didn't look annoyed, but I'm sure he gave me the slip. He'd gone to the bus station at the far end of the city and he stood there for two whole hours. There were buses on every route and everyone was getting on and off, coming and going, while he stood there like a statue. I left him and retraced my steps."

Kada spoke as if he were writing a detailed report for his immediate boss in the intelligence department. Ousmane La Gauche didn't hesitate to call him a big mouth, then he said to him, "Forget the trivial details and let's make a decision."

"Decide what?" asked Mubarak.

"I don't know," replied Ousmane in frustration.

That gave Kada another chance to resume speaking. He told them that after the previous day's session he had visited all the patients in bed in the city hospital, but none of them looked like the missing man. Then he went to see the cemetery guard and asked him, but he didn't have any information that was useful to the case. He emphasized the word "case," as if the most important man on the face of the planet had disappeared. "The burial couldn't be done without a signed permit. I found the guard half awake. Sometimes he takes pills," he told them.

Mubarak frowned when he heard that. "He never shows any sign of that!" he commented in surprise.

"Do you expect a man who lives in the middle of a cemetery to be wholly in his right mind?" replied Kada. "Anyway, he confessed to me that he does allow a friend of his to dig up graves that no one visits and take bones and stuff from them, to sell to sorcerers and charlatans. But 'burying someone without the authorities' knowledge,' as he put it, would be impossible, even if you'd swallowed the contents of a whole pharmacy. That's what he insisted." His upper body bent forward and his head bowed, he continued almost inaudibly: "I'll tell you a secret. I went to that woman. You know her, of course, don't pretend to be innocent, that old woman who procures women and girls. I described him carefully to her, and she said no man of that description had ever come to her."

Everyone at the table was at a loss, their thoughts going round and round in circles. Ousmane La Gauche cast doubt on the notion that the man had disappeared, without noticing that this meant casting doubt on the man's existence in the first place.

"I read the papers daily and I've never read about a suicide in our area or a report of a missing person," he said.

"But maybe he doesn't have a family to report him if he doesn't come home," commented Mubarak. "He used to go to the weekly market," he added, as if to assert that the man existed, that he was the only person who had ever seen him, and that the others were calling him a liar. "Several times I saw him carrying bags of fruit and vegetables. He used to visit my café every now and then. He certainly didn't have a stable job. He suddenly turned up here among us, as if he were born fully grown or fell from the sky. Maybe he'd always been among us but we didn't notice his presence and we were surprised only when he disappeared."

"That guy's a djinni," said an old man with a gray beard sitting not far behind them. "I heard everything you all said," he continued confidently, "Some of you might not believe me. As you like. But the guy you're looking for might be a djinni who lived among us for a year in the guise of a man. Then he went as he had come. Don't trouble yourselves. He's from the other world." The old man left them completely surprised and went back to browsing a sports newspaper.

One of the customers called over Mubarak to pay for a coffee he'd been sipping for an hour while also listening to them. Light rain outside had deterred Ousmane La Gauche from going out and he was still listening to what Kada had to say. Kada had decided to tell his boss he hadn't found out anything about the mysterious man, but in return he gave a commitment to come again and consult with Mubarak and Ousmane on everything related to the case. A short young man pushed the door open and came in carrying a large leather briefcase. His thick hair was slightly wet. Mubarak scowled when he saw him. He was an official from the tax department. La Gauche and Kada smiled vindictively, then they deftly slipped out of the café without paying for their drinks. When he left earlier, the imam had also neglected to pay for his tea, leaving the amount on account.

Books alone do not make someone an intellectual. A real intellectual has to have opinions too. How pathetic Ousmane was when he believed such things. People see culture as something very marginal. He had experience of them and knew how fake they are. In serious times they choose ignoramuses and opportunists. Ousmane had suffered at their hands several times. He had stood as a candidate in the municipal elections, at the top of a leftist party list, but the party hadn't won a single seat, in a council with more than thirty seats. It took a slap in the face like that for him to understand what "the blind masses" are like, he grumbled to Mubarak one day. Mubarak seconded what he said as if he really believed it. He appreciated why Ousmane was so aggrieved and understood what he had said about castrated intellectuals. The man was a drunkard, candid, and, in front of Mubarak, he lamented all the years he had spent dreaming of change. These people love people who herd them like camels, not people who convince them and teach them how to be their equals, he repeated sadly several times. Even his friends kept away from him. "Spare us the politics," they replied coldly when he asked them to share his dream, which would grow bigger. He didn't hold it against them. Maybe they had been dreamers like him until the real world chastened them and they learned not to break the rules. He vented his anger on the "blind masses," hypocritical and avaricious, who seek rulers with angelic dispositions while they themselves behave like devils. They deserve to be dominated by opportunists and people who exploit religion for financial or political gain. But he had washed his hands of all this. He just talked about it repeatedly in order to alleviate the serious disappointment he had suffered some years earlier.

The events of life had humbled him terribly. How many men have lived in an age that didn't deserve them? He was still sad about a failure he had tried his best to avoid. He had married a woman called Zahiya and withdrawn from the world. Then he had children and providing a decent life for his family became his greatest challenge. After the age of fifty, everything looks the same to a man who dreams and then fails and is then thoroughly defeated. When it was strong, generous, and grandiose, the state tended to spend money with great extravagance. Someone advised him to open a bookstore and stationer's. Providing stationery and other office supplies to government departments and schools could be very profitable. The goods were consumables, the accounting was lax, and the bills were always inflated. The idea tempted him and an instinctive greed stirred inside him. He wanted to make up for his years of poverty, and idealism could go to hell. Prophets don't have grandchildren or heirs who survive. People can plunder well-stocked warehouses and the state is content and lures them on to more. Zahiya was eager to be like her peers and he had been unable to buy her a single ring since they married fifteen years earlier. All he had given her was words. He had been thrown the scraps, and bad luck had pursued him, as a dreamer and as a thief. Before long Zahiya tried to discard him like a smelly pair of socks with holes. She rebelled against him. He beat her and spent the night somewhere else several times. He was wracked by suspicions and it hurt him that she had probably left him for another man who was more virile, that she had run away from an impoverished life with a man who couldn't afford Viagra pills and who spoke tediously about books and how the disjointed times had wronged the likes of him. "I want to live my life," were the last words he heard from her, in front of the female judge who looked like a man. She was about to disgrace him, so he preferred to cut his losses. She won her freedom by paying him a sum of money, but he never knew where she obtained it from, and he looked more subdued than he had ever been before. The pain remained alive in his heart forever. The children went to live with their grandmother and they visited him sometimes. The eldest child looked like her and there was a mean look in her eye that reminded him of Zahiya. He slapped her the first time when she told him that her mother seemed happy with her new husband and was learning to drive. He wanted her to tell him how sad and remorseful Zahiya was that she had left him and that if she could she would crawl back on her hands and knees. After that their visits were less frequent and then they ceased. In the end he believed he was dogged by bad luck, his heart was hardened, and he believed that the philosophical god he believed in had neglected him, tormented him in fanciful ways, and then abandoned him, weak and helpless, to his fate. He ended up running an illegal business in order to make ends meet. He completely abandoned his standards-based perspective on the world and his only concern was to be a success at something. He liked looking after the children even after they tried to avoid him. One day he beat his son with his trouser belt and left marks on his skin, then he sat next to him and cried. He was tempted to kill his former wife, but it was just an impulse and he didn't have the wherewithal to put it into practice. One day earlier he had seen her driving a car with her husband at her side and the sight made him seethe with anger. In the evening he went to the station district in a rage. He tracked down the young man who would later disappear and demanded the money he was owed. Forgetting's no excuse for not paying, he told him sharply. Yet he did sympathize with him. The man was an outsider like him, let down by himself and by his bitter life.

He complained to Mubarak like a child confiding his troubles to his father. Sometimes Mubarak felt sorry for him and sometimes he listened irritably. When he listened to him, Mubarak thought that they were close friends and that he could seek Ousmane's help in finishing off the plan that had kept him awake for so many years. Then he backed off, worried he might catch bad luck off a man that God crushed every day to punish him. Mubarak did have paternal feelings toward Ousmane. He had flights of imagination, then came back to his senses. God had not given him any sons and it was too late to change anything. His hesitation had been his undoing. He should have married another woman right after the death of his first wife, a tough woman who wouldn't have allowed him to take a second wife for any reason whatsoever. Otherwise he might have found a fertile young woman and then left it to God to decide whether he would have a son. What use is money to you now, Mubarak? He had started taking stock of his life with more courage than ever. His daughters' husbands would inherit his life savings, without gratitude or appreciation, and if any of them had a chance to piss on his grave after his death, they might well do so, in revenge for him having lived for so long that he had deprived them of his wealth. That was something he hadn't taken into account.

Ousmane put him in a bad mood with his repeated complaints about life. Mubarak left him and went off. So there he was, consumed with remorse, too old and gray to keep fighting with himself all the time. Mubarak performed the evening prayers, led by Cheikh Hassan, and went home dragging his feet, trying to hold down the questions inside him. But the questions kept coming up to the surface to nag him. What use is all the gold in the world if it's piled up in front of you? Wouldn't it be better to give each of his five daughters their share of his estate, to see the joy and gratitude in their eyes and keep their husbands at bay for the rest of his days? In fact, the best thing to do would be to go on pilgrimage to Mecca and have your sins forgiven. What would you say to God when he asks you? These were solutions that were sure to bring him contentment, but they were still difficult, and the most difficult aspect of it was that he had started thinking of going for broke—wondering if he should marry again at his age. He might have a son late in life, and only for a few years, but that would be better than dying with a painful sense that something was missing. With money he could buy everything. He would choose a beautiful plump young woman, a widow, or a divorcee who already had children. The courts were full of such women, poor women just looking for support. He asked which day was set aside for divorce cases in the Rouïba court. He went there two or three times and liked many of the women. He wanted to catch one and prayed to God to be kind to him. Although Ousmane warned him of the risks and he did have some second thoughts, he had in mind a woman in her forties, blonde and well built, from a poor family and with one child. He had found what he was looking for and was about to take the initiative, but he couldn't pluck up the courage at the end of the day. His daughters fell out with him when they heard of his intentions. The middle one, the one closest to his heart, made fun of him scathingly and advised him not to do anything scandalous before he died. "Die decent, dad," she said. What she said was harsh on him. He went home offended, and in the evening the other daughters gathered at his place to give him advice, as they claimed, while their husbands remained neutral on the surface. He listened to his daughters and they started reteaching him the end-of-life wisdom that had deserted him. They took turns serving him, cleaning the house, and cooking for him so that he would have no pretext for getting married. That's what they told him in unison. They understood what he wanted, and yet they persistently treated him as stupid and ignored his urgent desire to have a male child. His grandchildren were the children of those men who remained neutral and harbored a secret desire to dig his grave as soon as possible. His daughters went off and left him thinking, and there remained within him a resolve to do what he wanted to do. But your new wife would produce a boy for you and then kill you to get everything, Ousmane told him, frightening him. Ousmane continued, seeking clarification from him: "And, for a start, are you sure you're up to it?" Mubarak didn't answer him and that was what really made him back off for a time. Ousmane had confronted him with a question he had been avoiding. Ousmane enjoyed proving to himself that he wasn't the only one who had to confront the fact that he was now impotent.

Rafik Nassiri, the detective, listened to these men one by one, and they all gave useless answers. They concluded that the man who had disappeared signaled disaster and they should keep their distance. The only person who admitted he had spoken with the man more than once was Mubarak. He was one of my customers, and we have to speak with them, Mubarak said. Some of the men denounced Mubarak. He had been seen going to the old man's apartment several times. Mubarak would visit the mystery man and talk to him in the café when he came, and their conversations can't have been just small talk between a café owner and one of his customers. He had to admit some contact with the man, as long as it wouldn't drag him into trouble he would rather do without. He had accumulated his wealth dinar by dinar, protected himself from envious malcontents, and deprived himself of everything up till then. He had come from the countryside alone and hungry, with cracked skin on his bare feet. He couldn't afford a paltry pair of shoes. He had worked like an ox in the fields. Just so that the harvest of a lifetime should end up as plunder enjoyed by the lazy? What justice is there in this world? With all his heart he hoped that God would grant him a boy. He may have been a coward who loved money more than he ought—he fully understood that now. He blamed himself and resented the woman who had prevented him from marrying another woman. When he remembered her, he said the fires of Hell would consume her, God willing. Otherwise, by now he would have had a son the age of that young man or older. He had wanted to help him, and had decided to reveal his life's secret to him and ask him to share it because he wanted to treat him as the son that he hadn't been blessed with. Mubarak would have been happy when he saw that young man happy, as if he were his son, of his own flesh. He felt for him, whereas the man who had disappeared was an idiot who didn't understand him. That was the comment he made the last time he saw him. He led Ousmane and the others to believe he had a grievance against him because of the debt, so as not to raise their suspicions. But in his heart he really hoped to bequeath everything to him while he was alive. He would have told him he wasn't a slave that could be bought . . . stupid, okay, now he had suddenly disappeared, as suddenly as he had appeared, and his hope had been dashed.

7

The Compass of the Heart

A FAINT LIGHT SHONE THROUGH A crack in the window. Inside his car, in the local square, Rafik was monitoring any possible activity, but in no hurry to go up to the apartment, although it was already the third night he had spent on watch there, awaiting the reappearance of the man who had disappeared. The world is full of mysteries—real ones and fictitious ones, but what had really kept him busy over the past days was trying to find the missing man or at least find out what had happened to him. This time he arrived later than on the two previous nights. He saw that faint light coming from the sitting room, but he didn't budge an inch.

He knew the apartment. He had been inside it and searched it thoroughly. It was on the top floor and yet he remained hesitant to go up. The night was blacker than it should be. He kept his eyes wide open so that no one could go into or come out of the building under cover of darkness without him seeing them.

For some reason he had come to see the search for the missing man as a very personal matter, more important to him than anything else. He had lived deprived of things he could be interested in. There was his work, his car, his house, which was more like a fancy prison cell, his family in the west of the country, friends, playing sports. But all those things didn't always give his life any savor or meaning, and deep down he felt an emptiness that nothing could fill. But that wasn't the fatal defect. Most people live meaningless lives. Their lives may be full in many ways, yet they lack meaning. He would not lie to himself and say that he sympathized with the man, since he didn't know him and they had never met or exchanged friendly words. He didn't know whether the missing man was sane and in good health, or whether he was mentally deranged or had some incurable disease, or whether, with money he had earned working in fields or building sites, he had boarded a boat with other illegal migrants and the sea had swallowed them all up. Curiosity, or a desire to be defiant and uncover the man's secret, if he had a secret. He wasn't sure of anything about him, except that he would keep looking for him.

He asked for some compassionate leave but his request was rejected. He put in another request, accompanied by a report from a psychiatrist at the central police hospital, saying he needed to stay away from the pressures of work for a while so that he could work properly later. Any other officer could easily have accepted an unexpected failure such as this. Life is full of failures and a superman has never been born. Yet after resting for two days, he had decided to keep looking for the missing man on his own initiative.

He looked back and forth between the window and the door of the building and wondered what compelled him to fill his time doing all this. His room for maneuver was shrinking: the later it was, the more difficult it would be for him to go and take him by surprise in the apartment. He might make a noise or there might be a confrontation between them if the man thought he was a thief. He thought of phoning Kada to come and help him, then decided against it. It started to rain. Kada lived nearby but he had a thousand tricks he could use as excuses for not coming to help. Rafik knew him well: he was as slippery and unpleasant as a toad.

Was this a life or some kind of competition organized by fate? How many concessions does a man have to make in order to adapt and conform? Defeat and obligatory subjugation of the self are more polite than other terms and have less psychological impact, but the substance remains the same. Hoda contacted him and he didn't answer. She loved him and he worried about the effect his fate might have on her. His relationship with her was a task that was supposed to be complete, an effort at self-subjugation that had not yet produced any result. He loved her too, that's how he judged his feelings toward her at the time, and he would have been mortified if she had to make a sacrifice for his sake—that's what he expected and he couldn't deceive himself with the idealistic view that love works miracles. His previous experience taught him that love isn't everything. Hoda was already mother to a boy who would come to him ready-made and Rafik would adopt him as an antidote to his childlessness. He was about to fill the long-standing emptiness in his life, but then he decided against it and his journey came to an end only one stage after it began.

A love that is mature, that has come to terms with circumstances and that is half a sacrifice, might create a certain happiness. A happiness that is a quarter short of fulfillment. He had trained himself some time ago to challenge fate. Everything or nothing. It was a nihilistic logic but it would keep him as he was. Endless subjugation makes a travesty of one's self, so he decided to die as he was and not to be buried as a monster, and that was that. Hoda called again and he deliberately ignored her. In a text message she told him that his selfishness would be the end of him and she wouldn't make any sacrifices for his sake. The only things that would really kill the two of them were his delusions. She continued to trample on her own dignity, saying: please don't abandon me, let's be together and leave the rest to me. In response, he told himself there could be no more illusions. Consciousness is a form of torment, living powerless is double torment. A man like him, without recourse to drugs, has to swallow torment to the last drop. A cat hid under his car to get away from the wet, the cold, the night, and the loneliness. It started to meow to give voice to its loneliness, its sufferings under a light rain that had been falling since the afternoon. Its sufferings were probably pleasant: without consciousness anything is tolerable. The faint light was still on, the rain was falling lightly and sometimes pouring down. He felt the pointlessness of what he was doing. He was tired, drained, bracing himself to fill a deep abyss inside himself. He was tracking a man, but the traces had been almost completely erased. Maybe the mystery man was like him, a version braver than he was in refusing to submit or to pursue a life that didn't live up to his beginnings. He preferred to leave without a trace. He jumped into his inner abyss and wouldn't let anyone stuff him or weigh him down with endless trivialities. Here was fate offering him an example to emulate. He should learn from the man's disappearance and follow a different path in life, in order to end up, like the missing man, forgotten and at ease. Disappearing is more generous to one's self than a phony and deceitful existence with distorted features, where the lucky ones survive. No one mourns for rebels of his kind.

His patience wasn't limitless. He had expected a day would come when it ran out, and then it happened. He decided not to go on feeding his hopes with more empty delusions. It was clear he was sterile. The doctors claim to know everything. With the confidence of the ignorant, the last doctor he consulted had told him he had to be patient and he didn't have any physical problem. He had heard something similar from Mounira, his wife, when they came back from the doctor's. Reality is well able to show what's real, while hopes remain mere hopes. Was there hope after ten years? Mounira was generous with her patience and told him she liked living with him, with or without a child. She commiserated with him while he did his best to torment himself, taking her to stores that sold children's clothes and toys and wanting to buy a bicycle or a doll, or he would stop his car next to a kindergarten or a school and keep looking at the kids as they came out or went in. She often cried for their sake. He became the permanent object of her pity. They spoke little each time and their days passed drily and monotonously. Love isn't the cure for all problems. They understood that time would bring them closer together, but it is fruitful love alone that lasts long. She loved him. He didn't doubt that, but he didn't like to exploit her love for him any longer, and he didn't want her to pay the price for his bad luck before it was too late. You don't have the right to decide this on your own, Mounira said. She stated her objection, but he didn't reply. He thought her sacrifice for him was trivial. He loved her and protected her jealously. She was intelligent and she wouldn't remain a nun after him, and logically, in order to fulfill her maternal instincts, she would get over him and find another man. Jealousy has never killed a man, but childlessness, oh yes it has. Deeply hurt, he took the trouble to face her anger and then, sad and solicitous, he left her alone in the apartment to pack up her things at her leisure. In court she didn't ask him for anything. He felt relieved of the sense that he had wronged her in some way, and when he went back to the apartment at night he found it like a grave. He went back to being a bachelor, got used to living alone again, and never felt a moment's remorse, because he had saved her from his fate, albeit very belatedly.

He gave up waiting, out of necessity, and immersed himself in his daily activities. He felt relieved of the stress of looking into her eyes when he came home every evening, and of seeing in them an implicit accusation and hope that God would not deprive them of children forever. He signed up for a training course at the municipal swimming pool, bought various books, become more involved in work. He faced a double emptiness after divorcing her but he thought he had achieved some success. How had he allowed his passion for anything to play tricks on him again? Some stories begin with minor incidents. He slipped in the swimming pool and twisted his ankle, which required medical attention. In the hospital fate opened for him another door for a different form of waiting. He met Hoda Ouannas, a physiotherapist whose husband had died a year ago. He had left her with her boy Ouassim and some unpleasant memories. Less than a month after her husband's death, mourning him was just a mask she wore in the presence of others for the sake of appearances. Rafik thought he would finally have a child he could buy a bicycle for, a child he could adopt and whose company he could enjoy for a while. Half-deprivation is better than total deprivation. His divorced wife had suggested they adopt a child but he had flatly refused and replied accusingly that what she said about living with him even without children was nonsense. For your sake, she explained to him, we could ask my sister for her youngest daughter before she grows up and gets used to her, she added as he listened, embittered about everything. He wanted to get rid of her on the pretext that she shouldn't go without children because of him. This is what he admitted to himself on his first night after she left, and maybe he had noticed something in her eyes. She wasn't completely dismissive, her outburst was cold, he expected her resistance to be more forceful, and since she had left she hadn't called to ask to come back or to beg him to go back on his decision, or even to ask him how he was managing without her. He opened the door for her to go out of his life and she went out without looking back, as if she had just been waiting for the opportunity.

He had repeated meetings with Hoda, came to know her better, and fell in love with her. Her arrival on the scene helped him to understand that what had tied him to Mounira in the last years was obstinacy rather than real love. Hoda played chess very well. She beat him the first time they played in the hospital, and after that he never grew tired of being defeated by her—defeated as he always was, but this time when he was a king in her heart. Men have to go into the battles of love defeated from the start, otherwise their love won't succeed. He learned a new lesson from life. He almost forgot Mounira.

Memories of ten wonderful years could fade away and then be effaced completely. Hoda offered a whole emotional meal to his hungry heart, which was sated with emptiness and trivia and saw life as a dark block. His priorities changed, and straight after work he went to wait for her outside the hospital. He gave her a ride to her family's apartment or she came out to see him and they spoke a little and then she went back for her night shift. He followed her Facebook page and resented anyone who, unaware of the fires raging in his heart, gave a "like" to a picture of her. He would accuse her of flirting with her Facebook contacts, and she would laugh at him, and with a single conversation they could feel they were twenty years younger. He remembered Mounira and her severity, her measured behavior, her morbid obsession with cleanliness, and her smiles calculated to suit every situation. She was serious and more logical than she should be. He liked the spontaneity of the chess-playing doctor, her flexible attitude toward life, and how she wasn't a prisoner to the past in any way at all. He had to go along with her and drop his act as a policeman, a detective who looked into everything. With her he had to let the world take its course in the way she liked to run it. She was better at the art of life than him and he gave her free rein in everything. Her son Ouassim didn't take to him as well as he might. She told him that "Uncle Rafik" was like a father to him, but the young boy rejected the comparison, while Rafik complained that she was singing the praises of her late husband to him. He wanted her to see him as distinctive and special, just as he saw her as the kind of woman that a man might not meet more than once in a lifetime. Love wears tinted spectacles.

They got married quietly and he waited for her to finish off some things before she moved in to live with him. Finally he started to look forward to something other than children. No one has everything, that's what he convinced himself. He did up his apartment as best he could. He removed Mounira's severity and her schoolmarmish touch. Then it was ready to receive a woman like Hoda, who lived life with as little forethought as possible. They inspected the apartment. He remembered by heart the things she asked to be changed, and they merged like any couple. She spoke to him about colors, curtains, the kitchen, and the living room, and finally about the bedroom. He spoke to her about his love. He looked deep into her eyes, melted into her, and they had sex earlier than they had planned, since they hadn't had their wedding party yet. It was a little early, but also belated, given the highly charged glances they had exchanged since the first day they met. Overwhelming elation. That night he told her how happy he was with her and how he had always hoped that when they were together they would produce a child. She was offended and responded more harshly than she appreciated at the time. "I'm not a breeding machine," she said. Their love shrank, diminished. They were silent for seconds before she left. He had hoped she would want to make him happy. Love isn't everything. She didn't understand that at the time. She apologized to him in the morning, but when she moved on to talk about other things, his silence showed he was sad and frustrated. That day, maybe, he decided not to take his dreams too far, to act his age again and leave it to fate alone to run his life. He came to terms with his childlessness and kept his dignity intact. A chess player might not be much good for love. She needed to lose to him sometimes and obey him even if he was misguided, mistaken, a dreamer who followed the word of doctors and resisted the clear will of God. In order to be king over the chessboard of her life, he would sweep everyone else away, so that in the end she would submit to him alone.

It was midnight and he didn't notice when the rain stopped. The cats fell silent, succumbing to the stillness. He watched a silhouette on the balcony right opposite Mourad's apartment as it appeared and disappeared. He thought it was probably someone with insomnia. He nodded off and his eyelids drooped. Then he opened his eyes to see two spectral figures coming out of the building. They disappeared within a few seconds. Maybe it was just a dream or maybe he just hoped that three whole nights on watch would produce something more than a meager harvest. He would have followed the two figures if he hadn't seen them at a time when he was half-way between waking and sleeping. The rain and the darkness didn't help. The streetlights were faint and some of them had burned out. He got out of the car, walked a few steps, and then stopped. He found himself in the middle of an open space with cars parked in lines along the sides. Nothing but him. He looked up at the window and saw that the light had gone out. He felt belittled and powerless toward the stupid situation he had put himself in. You should have burst into the apartment, he said in exasperation, reproaching himself. Then he had second thoughts and wondered whether the person inside was the person he was looking for. But he had seen two figures coming out of the building and then disappearing, not just one . . . Had he really seen anything? He turned and saw the silhouette on the balcony, opening the shutters wide. He was sure it was a woman. There was something he didn't understand. His watch showed it was twenty minutes past midnight. He played around aimlessly, reread Hoda's messages on his phone. He drove off, determined not to go back there again. His enthusiasm hadn't waned, but he had reconsidered his approach. The search for that man had to resume somewhere else. Aimlessly, he drove around the almost deserted streets of Rouïba for a whole hour, going over everything he had heard about him and what he had managed to find out about him. He tried to imagine what he looked like. He wished he could meet him without any preconceptions. They would have a chat and he could learn from him how someone can erase almost all the signs of their existence. Did he really exist? He was born just like anyone else. He had parents and a family. He went to school and the teacher punished him because he hadn't finished his homework. He grew up and harassed girls in the street. He desired women and masturbated in his adolescence, then he grew older and was dumped by a woman who didn't deserve him. He couldn't afford to enjoy life in the same way as his friends did. He went to the barber's, he had fights with friends on the beach, he watched soccer matches, and sometimes he was reckless and made countless stupid mistakes. He graduated from university and lived frustrated, filled with rancor against the damned government, so he tried to emigrate illegally by boat. All of this or none of it, and he did almost all of it, so why did he feel that it made almost no difference whether he existed or not?

In this country corruption is rampant. It's part of people's lives and they have grown used to it. It's a whole philosophy of government. The state is pretty much a giant free-for-all. That's what he heard from his friend the last time they spoke. His friend was frustrated and decided to emigrate to Canada. He said goodbye to Rafik and urged him to join him soon. On the edge of the city, when he drove past on his night tour, he saw the piece of land that had caused him so much trouble. His car itself, and what happened to it, showed that their threats were much more serious than he had expected. Some big shot had appropriated part of the piece of land, which had been allocated to a farmer as a franchise. The big shot was planning to build a hotel and night club. Out of fear or because he was complicit, the farmer who held the lease made no objection. Preparations began and the foundations were laid, although building permits had been completely suspended in the capital. A routine patrol by the building police filed a report for submission to the courts. One sunny Friday morning he had parked his car and gone to a sauna to relax. While he was there, someone emerged through the steam to tell him that his car had been smashed up, and the next day the commissioner summoned him to find out what had happened. A large-circulation newspaper picked up the story. Where had they gotten the details from? Respect for the law should not stand in the way of a good deed, so he had called an old friend from student times who worked as a journalist, Soufiane Thabti, who was one of the free voices campaigning against the tide of public corruption. Rafik told him what had happened and a story was published. A committee of inquiry from the provincial administration was dispatched, building work on the hotel was stopped in the early stages, and the lease was withdrawn from the farmer. Excellent steps, unless they were merely part of a tit-for-tat feud between rapacious people intent on plunder. A senior official had lost out on some deal and sought revenge on his rivals. The incident suited his purposes and through it he was able to do his rivals down. The provincial governor suspected Rafik, though he didn't have any proof he had leaked anything to the press. The gangs fought, struck out at each other, and they didn't lack sources of information they could use as weapons against their rivals. He had won one round, at least that's what he thought, but Mounira advised him not to stand in the lion's mouth. Courage alone is not enough. He knew she was right but her advice came too late. Days passed and someone asked to meet him. He went downstairs from his office and there were two men waiting. They said it was a private matter "if you would be so kind," and he set off with them toward a nearby café. One of them spoke to him with exaggerated politeness. They walked some distance from the police station and before they reached the café the tone began to change. You'll pay the price, said the man, who abandoned his civility and whose eyes bulged, while the other broke his silence to warn him that "he had dug his own grave." They got into a fancy car that was waiting for them and left him standing on the pavement. After that he realized that smashing up his car was just a token gesture, and the next day Mounira's car disappeared from outside their building. She reminded him that she had already warned him. She had to walk to the secondary school where she taught for a week, until her father bought her another car. That day he called Soufiane Thabti and, judging by his voice, Soufiane seemed to regret having challenged them. They were a real mafia, he said. Everything has a price, Rafik replied, and then Soufiane advised him to ask for a transfer from Rouïba to somewhere else in the capital until the affair was forgotten.

Some time passed after the incident. The security director-ate opened an inquiry, the purpose of which was not exactly intelligible, but it was clear someone important stood behind the person whose interests had suffered and was protecting him. This was just speculation but it turned out to be true: building work on the hotel resumed and the concrete framework rose as if nothing had happened. In the meantime Rafik asked to take his annual vacation and obtained approval immediately. He kept away from work and separated from Mounira and then had more time for Hoda, until the commissioner called on him exceptionally after the old man's body was found in the apart-ment in the station district. But Rafik no longer paid attention to anything. The mischievous child and then the ambitious stubborn young man that he had been had both disappeared, clearing the way for the apathy that had overwhelmed him. Lions can't be milked, but they can be tamed and can perform in the circus to amuse the naïve and the cowardly. He would die before that happened. So he would just end up waiting, nothing but waiting, and yet he was really lucky. If he had had a child, they could have broken his heart by harming the child.

It was one hour short of dawn. Frustrated, he went home to sleep. He wished he could lose himself in a place where no one recognized him, and where he had forgotten his child-lessness and disappointment. Ever since he was young he had been accused of loving heroism and showing off. Moments before falling asleep, his greatest wish was to disappear or become invisible, to fade away and not leave any trace of him-self, as the man who had become Nobody had managed to do, achieving complete heroism.

8

Pure Fate

ANXIETY IS A LETHAL POISON, and life is a sure recipe for torment. Ousmane La Gauche's life had never been this bad
before. He had to submit to the absurd calculations that life
imposes. The world couldn't stand on one leg. The left alone
wasn't enough. He accepted that. He had shat out all his old
convictions and was content to live like a wolf. But now he
was a poisoned victim, powerless and abhorrent. Damn all
those who are unable to act, whatever the reasons might be.
He stood there drunk, watching Zahiya. He didn't know why
he was following her or rubbing salt into his own wounds by
watching her. The stationery shop was still closed and he had
free time to monitor her activities. He saw Zahiya come out
of her husband's villa and drive off in a car worth at least ten
times as much as he could afford. Her husband, the stupid
old man, spent lavishly on her, and seemed happy with her.
Maybe he thought his new wife was the ideal woman. Where
did he first see her and how did she meet him, since she didn't
go out of the house? Did she bewitch him? He was worried
she might notice his presence nearby. She had threatened
him with the police when he approached her one time. She
had given up her husband and children for the sake of her
own pleasure. A loose woman, a cow—all the insults in the
world wouldn't allay his anger. He went home to drink, or to
Mubarak's café to ask dozens of questions without taking the
trouble to seek the answer to any of them. Could that old man

satisfy her hunger in a way that he couldn't do himself? The man was older than him and further advanced along the road to decrepitude. Maybe he'd found some secret concoction or some amazingly effective pills. No. Only money performs miracles. She looked at Ousmane with contempt. He insisted on harassing her, and once he heard her say, "I'll speak to you one day." She wanted to fob him off. He didn't get the message, so she threatened to file a complaint against him.

She told him in haste that she had never hated him, but she wanted to save herself and her children. His curse would have struck them all, so she had to act. Ousmane asked Kada to help and he made inquiries about her. Her new husband had set up a big garment workshop for her, arranged for twenty seamstresses to work there, and placed a large deposit in her bank account, and so she had become important, in a way. Zahiya had once told him she was thinking of applying for one of the microloans set aside for women who stay at home so that she could buy a sewing machine. He dragged his feet and snuffed out her enthusiasm for the idea. But she had finally found someone who appreciated her talent for sewing and would help her achieve her dream. Once Kada tried tempting Ousmane into blackmailing her but Ousmane said, "I would never accept a bribe. Unlike her, I'm not the kind that runs after money." Zahiya was cured of poverty and had taken off like a rocket, while he just rolled around in the mud like a mangy dog. Ousmane's son Oualid told him that Zahiya's new husband did everything she asked of him and for her sake he had fallen out with all his own children. Ousmane burned with anger whenever Oualid told him some new detail of her new life. He seriously considered hitting Oualid when he saw the effect his rival's generosity had on his son, but he backed off at the last moment and didn't utter even one word of disapproval. But fatherhood is not a matter of words. The children loved only her and avoided visiting him. They had no need for a useless father like him, a failure and a drunk.

The interloper took control of everything, while he lost his family because he was a man of principle and had bad luck. He called an old school friend, Ashour the postmaster, but Ashour didn't reply. Ashour ignored him and avoided meeting him. Ousmane eventually asked Ashour to lend him some money and he gave a feeble excuse for refusing. He wasn't a real friend, or else he would have helped him, at least to find a job. Ashour knew lots of people but his sympathy for Ousmane wasn't sincere. Ousmane had given him so much help in exams. Ashour was a jackass and didn't understand a thing. When they were at school together, Ashour would pay for cigarettes and sandwiches while Ousmane copied out the lessons, explained them to him, did the homework, and fed the answers to him during exams if the proctor was distracted. Ousmane danced at Ashour's wedding and was very happy for him, but then Ashour insulted him in front of the guests. He made them laugh at Ousmane by saying he was slow-witted and idealistic. Ousmane kept his distance for a while but was soon appeased by a trivial apology. Ousmane had a long history of feeling inferior, though later he tried to make up for it a little. He restored some of the balance in his relationship with Ashour, and yet nothing lasts. Affection is too weak to withstand the tests of time and fates at cross purposes. Ashour left him in suspense for two days, then offered him a 1,000-dinar note and he had no choice but to accept it. Ousmane became very withdrawn. All the things he used to talk about endlessly no longer had any importance. Intellectuals were just plucked chickens drowning in their own shit. Only full pockets impose their logic. He no longer had access to supplies from the beer factory so, after selling booze without the government's knowledge, he went bankrupt and could hardly afford his own daily bread. To make a living he put copies of the Quran back in his bookshop, along with books on fatwas and copies of Malik's *Muwatta'*. His bookstore didn't provide even a subsistence income and most of what he earned went to rent for the store.

No one reads these days and ignorance is spreading like the plague. He owed the landlord three months' rent on the store. The landlord was threatening to evict him and, as a last resort, had given him one week to pay up. His other business, selling alcohol, had covered his needs, but now he was completely destitute and his ex-wife added to his misery and wore him down. He thought she should pay the price, any price.

He sat down with Mubarak, the person closest to him in recent times, and spoke to him at length in a low voice. This time Mubarak didn't grumble about hearing the story repeated. In the story of his friend's misfortune he found some consolation for what he was going through himself, even if what he faced wasn't quite so tragic. The previous evening had been a turning point: he had faced the difficult test and emerged triumphant. The rain had stopped and after midnight he was coming out of the apartment of the dead man's son and going down the stairs in the building in a state of elation. He wasn't completely unlucky, his fears had abated, and he still had hope. If it turned out that Ousmane had asked him about his sexual capabilities only to embarrass him and to prove to himself that he wasn't the only impotent man around, he could boast that he had successfully passed the test and proven he still had some virility left. His heart was no longer young and taking those pills all the time would tire him out. He needed two years at the most to see the baby boy in front of him, then he could say goodbye to the world with his mind at rest. The young woman had tired him out. He would never find out that she had kept the blue shirt as a special token since he didn't intend to repeat the experience. He had decided to embark on what was useful. His face looked tired but he looked satisfied with himself in a way, and angry with himself in that he had allowed his late wife to ruin his health. Even after her death he had hesitated to seek another wife for a long time and his courage and his principles let him down several times. Hellfire would inevitably consume him, but that was something for the future. On the Day of Judgment he would find out how God would respond, to hold him to account for fornicating at such an advanced age. He had never been promiscuous but circumstances had imposed it on him. And what now? He repeated the question to himself, and Ousmane left him to his silence. Let the daughters go to hell, they're nasty and they inherited envy and greed from their mother. He would die with his reputation intact to spite them all. Only the woman who produced a baby boy for him would deserve all the wealth he had accumulated over his lifetime. He went and asked Cheikh Hassan about it. He did the kind of thorough ablution necessary after committing a serious sin and performed the dawn prayers, then he sat with the sheikh in his section of the mosque. The sheikh met his question with a smile and then clasped Mubarak's hand and encouraged him. "Make a vow to trust in the Lord," he told him. When you're trying to save what can be saved, you mustn't take sacrifices into account or make petty calculations. He didn't regret the amount he had paid to Kada and his friend Djelal the bleary-eyed cemetery janitor for arranging the woman and the place. Because of the partial success he had achieved, he wouldn't consider the money he had paid to be a serious loss. Kada had opened up Mourad's apartment for him and brought the woman so that he could see if he was up to it. He hadn't done that for years—he had wasted his life but it wasn't the right time to lament or recover the fitness that had been destroyed by inactivity and old age. He would renovate the house and order his daughters to help him and they would obey. Fear and greed would motivate them and they wouldn't rebel against him. He had seen that poor woman in her forties and his heart went out to her. She left the courtroom with her father and he followed them and took her father's phone number. Then he made an appointment with him and visited them at home. She had one five-year-old daughter, who could stay with her grandmother. He understood that the man was chronically poor and it was a foregone conclusion that he would agree to let him marry his daughter. He had made up his mind not to die without a male heir, after living his life without a son to help him, and whatever he left would rightfully belong to the woman who achieved his lifelong wish, and he wouldn't begrudge anything to a child he had long awaited. Ousmane stood up but Mubarak didn't even notice. He dismissed all Ousmane's warnings out of hand. She was a good woman and she wouldn't wrong him or disgrace his bed. All he had to do was pray to God to make sure he lived a little longer and that his heart held out so that the baby boy would come. He would be delighted to see him and then he could die without any regrets and as content as if he had obtained everything he wished for in this world.

By arranging Mubarak's encounter Kada had carried out another mission with success and he could relax for a whole day. On the next day he went to the café and found it shut. Mubarak's phone didn't answer. Ousmane didn't want to keep him as a permanent customer. Mubarak's heart was weak and some woman might kill him and Kada could get caught up in it. His major prize was somewhere else. He waited for him outside his house for an hour, but to no avail, and his suspicion became a certainty. Every week Mubarak went away for a day or two and then reappeared. This time might be decisive. He hoped his calculations weren't mistaken. If luck was on his side and his plan succeeded, it would be the greatest thing that could happen to him, and he would be cured of his misery for the rest of his days. It wasn't so much that he wasn't resourceful, more that his luck worked against him. He had stayed up the night before with Djelal in the cemetery, just the two of them, far from the domino-playing rabble. They smoked two joints and got talking. Djelal ended up proving a truth that was blatantly obvious to him in his reduced state of consciousness. His eyes stuck out and he looked as if he were going to tell Kada some deep secret: "Kada, you're common.

If God really loved me, he would have provided me with a better friend." The other man replied in cold blood: "We're all riffraff, my friend. I'm corrupt by nature while you're a chancer and one of the most despicable people in the world. You sell the bones of the dead and support your mother and your brothers on the proceeds from their remains." Djelal nodded in agreement, then added by way of clarification: "They stole our lives and our souls while we were still alive. I think it's very fair that I should take revenge on them when they're dead." Their cigarettes were about to burn out and they fell silent, and everything they had said, like the smoke, blew away in the wind. They were like two mirrors, two bare images, two men reconciled to their truths forever. The dead at rest nearby weren't upset by their chitchat or their vulgar language. The dead have nerves of steel and are more patient than any of the living. The old madame, the mistress of the profession, as Kada called her, the woman with the blue nightshirt, the new den of iniquity . . . The two of them stayed up chatting by the light of a lantern, like bugs at night drawn to a faint light. Kada visited Djelal whenever something new came up. This time he came out of Djelal's place after asking him to be on standby. This time we might need a new grave or we might open a forgotten grave that no one has visited, he said. Djelal, who was lying on his side, stood up when he heard that. "Why? Are you planning to hide someone's body?" he asked. Kada didn't reply. Djelal was silent for a while then he continued: "Didn't you ask me that before and you promised me lots of money, and then nothing happened?" Kada tried to reassure him as he walked off: "Don't worry. This time luck will be on my side." And then, with great confidence: "You'll get your share. It will be the deal of your life, you grave robber."

Kada went back home and lay on his bed in an apartment with one bedroom, a kitchen, and a bathroom. The municipality had given him the place on the recommendation of a security agency, in return for his services. Productive work as an informer. He was bored of all that. His eyes were still wide open, staring at the ceiling, a little tired from staying up late the day before, and looking forward to his next opportunity. He had received a reasonable amount of money from Mubarak, at a serious cost to his own dignity, and he had to put an end to this degradation. People are bastards and the ones who win are the biggest bastards of all. Who would have expected he would end up where he was? At the July 5 Stadium, back in the 1990s, he had chanted with the crowds. He was one of those who had shouted at the top of their voices. "Islamic! Islamic!" and "By the profession of faith we live, by it we die, and by it we meet God," they had said. That was when he was a young man starting out in life. God had a place in his heart. He had been detained with all the others and the tyrants had triumphed in their war against the Islamic awakening. God had let them down, abandoned them as easy prey for the military. There were plenty of hypocrites and God has no obligation to help everyone and his uncle just because they have spoken out in public in the name of Islam. The times changed and people forgot them. Inside Berrouaghia prison he saw hell with his own two eyes. He was tortured and abused and he had wanted to die, and yet he continued to believe in the Islamic Salvation Front. Some of its leaders were imprisoned and others escaped and were pursued. Some of them turned out to be frauds and took the side of the tyrant regime. In spite of everything, he had suffered and endured. One cold night they had huddled together to keep warm. The cell was freezing and smelled moldy. They were held separately until the prison authorities put some highly dangerous common criminals in among them. They had some difficult times with them. He heard that in other cells criminals of this kind were trying to spread their deviant practices to the other inmates. They groped each other's asses and whispered to each other. Someone who didn't seem to care would suddenly break down in tears. Someone else would piss in his pants. Their hearts grew insensitive or they were afraid of something he didn't know about. They had banal conversations, they reconsidered their beliefs and remembered their children, then cried bitterly. Was it psychological warfare on the part of the prison administration or was it for real? He didn't reach any conclusive answer. His resistance broke down. Endless humiliation. He was shocked by what he heard. Wasn't it for the sake of these people that he had raised the banner of God, to save them from the plague of atheism and despotism? It was called the Islamic Salvation Front, but to save who and at what cost? One officer spoke to him and he listened with his head bowed in shame, when once he would bow only to his Lord. Something inside him was broken and after that he couldn't lift up his head. He was of a delicate constitution and couldn't bear to be subjected to any humiliation for too long. He showed he was prepared for anything and from that day on the word "no" disappeared from his lexicon forever.

He came out of prison and made more and more concessions till there was nothing left to concede. After all those years, who could he possibly choose as a target for vengeance? He was a loathsome man, willing to commit any outrage in return for money, and in his absence they called him an informer. Brother Kada Bensafia came to be called Kada the Informer. He ignored that. He knew he was hated like a pig with no pride, but there was no way he could change his image. Several times he tried to make a new start, in another city with different people. The remains of his dignity stirred, then died down again. He was stuck in a hole that was hard to get out of. People aren't completely innocent or necessarily more honorable than him. They are varied and wear a thousand masks. They are opportunists like him, maybe more so. What distinguished him from them is that he showed his true face, didn't beat about the bush, serving his own interests and not claiming to be moral. He didn't grow a beard, stand in the front line in the mosque, lie to God, or keep anything to himself. He lied to unfortunate people and took advantage of their situation. He sent loose women to those who asked for them and received payment from both parties. He was a thief and a wanderer, a liar and a tattletale, a walking ragbag of evils, but no one ever accused him of hypocrisy. One ordeal would be enough to turn him back into a freak. If he had been a true believer, he would have waited patiently and wouldn't have ended up the way he was. He heard them whispering about him to each other in the neighborhood and laughing. A police dog, a quisling who informs on his neighbors and the local people, probably without payment or in exchange for a pittance. If only he could tear up his CV and start again from scratch. He tossed and turned and tried to sleep, but the noise and the light at the end of day wouldn't let him doze at all. He started thinking about a new adventure, the chance of his lifetime if he made good use of it. The darkness started to descend and he decided to sleep early that night. He ate two eggs and some chicken breast left over from the previous day's meal. He went back to bed and threw himself down without changing his clothes. A few minutes later Rafik Nassiri called him on his phone.

Rafik wanted to meet up with him and had called to arrange it. Kada didn't reply and wasn't curious to know what Rafik was calling about. Rafik didn't know that such a meeting would never take place, even if he was certain from the start that nothing important would come of it. He had come back from Serdj El Ghoul disappointed. He had gone there without telling anybody, except for one colleague from his intake year in the police who worked there and promised to meet him when he arrived and to help him. Rafik was like a lost man, looking for something he had lost. He did obtain some real information about the missing man for the first time, but it was very much too late. It was true that as an adolescent there was nothing to distinguish the missing man from his peers. He was shy and too reserved for his age at the time. He lost his mother and then his father, and then his uncle and aunt looked after him. He was kidnapped at random in revenge for the murder of a soldier close to Serdj El Ghoul. He miraculously survived, and some people still talked about what happened to him. Rafik spoke to many people, and no one mentioned that they had seen him after the incident, so did he really survive, Rafik wondered, after hearing two people say that he had died and that the rumor of his survival was spread by a man known for his bloodthirstiness at the time, in order to claim a heroism he didn't deserve. Uncle Saleh, as they called him, the man who was said to have saved him, later became the head of the town council. He had passed away, but his son told the two of them that his father had told him that on one of his visits to the capital he had met, by chance in a pizzeria, a young man he had saved him from certain death during the civil war. The missing man's brother, Ammar, had left Serdj El Ghoul some years earlier. Rafik got hold of his number and with difficulty he managed to speak to him. Ammar said he hadn't seen his brother since their aunt died in the capital.

Rafik's car broke down on the road and he wasted a day. When he arrived he stayed in the Hotel Frantz Fanon in the center of Sétif. He took a short walk, went into the shopping mall, and early in the morning he went to Serdj El Ghoul to ask after the missing man. On his way back to the capital his mind couldn't make anything out of all the elements he had gathered. The family house, a property that was unregistered, had been bought by a teacher, a newcomer to the area who had now retired and didn't know anything about the people who had been living there before him. Some of the neighbors he asked told him that Ammar was Ibrahim's only child. If there was another child, no one had seen him and maybe he didn't exist in the first place. Some people have to lie to hide the fact that they know nothing about what they're being asked. The saddle-shaped mountain that overlooks the small town and gave the town its name—"The Ghoul's

Saddle"—invites everyone who looks at it "to mount the horse of the impossible" from time to time, or to disappear until they are nobodies. Rafik sat with his old colleague in a café, preparing to leave and filled with despair about the futile search. An elderly taxi driver came in and sat smoking a cigarette. He looked exhausted. He ordered a coffee and seemed unconcerned about anything. Rafik's colleague invited him to sit with them and asked him questions without expecting any special information. The man spoke at length about Ibrahim, who had been his dearest friend, and about his sister who had married her cousin and left, and about their brother. Rafik listened to him, gave him his full attention. I may be old but I have a good memory, the taxi driver told them. Once he had driven a man and his wife to the capital, to the Drid Hocine Hospital to be precise, and there he had seen a young man who looked exactly like Ibrahim. "You're the son of Ibrahim from Serdj El Ghoul," he had said to him, to check that his hunch was well founded. The man didn't reply. He seemed to be in a daze, speaking in whispers to a fat nurse and looking around in every direction as if he were frightened of something. He later went back to the hospital with Ammar and they asked after Ammar's brother, but the hospital management said he had recovered and the doctor had given him a discharge permit. They offered a bribe to the guard, and his tongue wagged. The man you're looking for had been accused of a crime. His name had come up in the case by mistake. Probably it was a groundless charge or someone had maliciously denounced him. Then the matter was sorted out. It was mistaken identity or maybe he really was a criminal, but no one could get any sense out of him. He escaped from the hospital on the night the doctor had agreed to discharge him, for fear of imprisonment or for some other reason that no one knew. The guard ended his story as if he had memorized it specifically to repeat to Ammar and the taxi driver. The nurses at the hospital didn't tell them anything about a fat colleague of theirs who had been sent for questioning, and whose address the hospital management had refused to reveal. But they did smile knowingly at each other when they were asked about her.

9

A Narrow, Crowded Path

MANY DAYS PASSED MONOTONOUSLY, AND it never occurred to Hoda the chess player to give up, not once. She wanted to have Rafik triumph over her superficially, so that she could win him over in the end. She understood the need to give him a chance to relax and catch his breath. Then, with as little scheming as possible, as was her constant habit, she would again surround him with her love. She busied herself with work, with Ouassim, and with defeating the man who challenged her on a chessboard where she could maneuver like no one else. She didn't try to contact him or send him messages by phone or on Facebook. Her intuition led her astray and she chose the wrong timing. She was a victim of the unknowable and things she couldn't foresee. She kept a copy of the keys to their apartment and she could have burst in on him at any moment, to declare her overwhelming desire to be defeated by him, and then save him from his delusions. But that was hardly something she intended to do in the immediate future. She preferred to wait. Many things passed her by in the days when she decided to catch her breath. Time does not wait for anyone. What fate had he chosen for himself, or had others chosen for him? He spent one night in his apartment, which he had prepared for her and from which he had removed Mounira's severity and schoolmistressy touch. He was seen coming out of the building on the morning after his return from Serdj El Ghoul. He went to the hospital to ask about an inmate who had been there some years back. He spoke with the manager, who received him hospitably at first, though his expression changed when he mentioned the man's name to him. They remembered the story very well there. The man had recovered and the doctor in charge of his case had given him permission to leave, the manager said. But he wouldn't reveal the name of the nurse who was investigated because of the escape incident and who was later moved to another hospital. She was going to get married soon and there was no need to cause her trouble by harking back to an old case. That was the last thing he heard from the manager. He left the manager's office when the manager pretended to be busy with an important phone call. The trip to Serdj El Ghoul had tired him out without producing anything useful. It may have brought him closer to Mr. Nobody, as he now called his counterpart. It certainly made him identify with him, and he had written lots of interesting observations about him in the small blue notebook he always carried with him, in a bag hung over his shoulder. Nothing weighed on his mind any longer. He handed in his service pistol at the police station since he no longer needed it. The commissioner called him to ask how he was and then told him they had reopened the investigation into the hotel case that had led to him being temporarily reassigned. Rafik showed only mild interest. He had got over that and his priorities had changed, though he did want to vent his anger in revenge, for the country, for everyone and for everything beautiful that had been ruined simply by greed and underlying evil.

He tried to call Kada on the phone but Kada didn't answer. A week later he no longer needed him and had forgotten why he had wanted him. He went to Mubarak's café in the afternoon and found it half-empty. A young man who was often yawning was in charge of serving the customers, and there was no sign of the others. He wondered what had brought him back to the station district, given that Mr. Nobody had disappeared and left no trace. He had killed Suleiman Bennaoui by a method that the incompetent forensic pathologist hadn't been able to identify, and then the pathologist had written that stupid report of his. Maybe Rafik was imagining this in order to frame the missing man on a false charge. He resented him and envied him because he couldn't emulate him, since Mr. Nobody was still among the living, even if the argument that he was visibly present was now untenable. His friend who had recently escaped to Canada, Soufiane Thabti, was pressing him to join him. He spoke to him about his ambition to become a brilliant journalist, in a country where there were no limits to human dreams. Rafik endorsed what he said and then complained that his life no longer had any importance worth mentioning. Before that he had visited the dead man's apartment. It was empty, though filled with the smell of death, as if the owner had died only yesterday. Everything was coated in dust and there were insects in the far corners. As for Mourad's apartment, there were clear signs that someone had passed through recently. No one but Rafik had the key to it, so had Mourad come back? Had he felt guilty? Had he wanted to say sorry but when he arrived, he discovered it was too late? Or else the real owner of the apartment, who had left it through a scandal, had come back, settled back in, and forgotten to change the lock on the door? He didn't want to consider the possibility that Mr. Nobody had gone back on his decision to vanish permanently and had passed by again. He had wasted a valuable opportunity on the day he saw the light on in the sitting room window but hadn't gone upstairs to take the person or people inside by surprise. He opened the balcony door and stood there for some minutes, then looked out to the balcony opposite. It was closed, and there was no silhouette looking out from it at anything. Then he went down to the café and within minutes a woman in her forties turned up there, sad and tense, and Rafik understood that she was Mubarak's daughter. Rafik had asked the yawning waiter about Mubarak but the waiter hadn't told him anything useful. Mubarak's phone was turned off and maybe he would turn up by nightfall or the next day. You women always exaggerate, he regularly disappears for a day or two every week, he heard the waiter tell her, but she objected to the rude way he spoke to her and thought that something unfortunate had probably happened to her father. Mubarak would lock up the café and go to visit his parent's grave at Chellalat El Adhaoura, and when his daughters asked him why he kept making the long journey every week he would pray to God to have mercy on his parents. To them he looked devout, as befitted a man who knew the duty of loyalty. But this time he had made the trip and hadn't taken the key to the café from the yawning young man and hadn't given any instructions to him or to his daughters. He had been absent a long time, and his daughters were anxious, while his plump and fertile wife had prepared everything in the expectation that she would move into his house and fulfill his life's dream. With a generosity that wasn't his usual practice he paid her a dowry as if she were a virgin and as if this was his first experience of marriage.

Rafik thought he had been selfish with Hoda. He loved her for his own sake and had then abandoned her when he felt like it, without taking into account the way she felt toward him. He stayed in the café some more minutes and spoke to his mother. He wasn't in the habit of troubling his mother with his problems, but this time he confessed to her that his life was now so empty it was pitiful. You need a child, Rafik, she said. She recited a long prayer for him, and then he asked her to forgive him whatever happened. But Mr. Nobody, who had disappeared from life only to live on in his anxious thoughts, was persistently suspected of being alive. Rafik hadn't died and he hadn't been killed. He was alive in a sense, or he wanted to die without letting go of life. He watched life from afar as if it didn't concern him and laughed at everyone else. He left the café for an unknown destination and at the door he met Ousmane La Gauche. He hadn't seen him since Suleiman Bennaoui had died. They exchanged glances quickly without saying hello. Ousmane struck him as someone whose life was coming to a painful and unexpected end. Ousmane had also come to ask after Mubarak and to offer to help him in any possible way, in order to extract from him any amount of money, however insignificant. The landlord at the bookstore had evicted him after the one week's notice had expired without him paying the rent that was due, and he really couldn't find anything to eat. Mubarak had been generous to him in recent days. He hadn't asked him to pay for the drinks he had had in the café and he had bought him local cigarettes two or three times. The last time he was at his place Mubarak had rewarded him with a hearty meal when he helped him move a new bed he had bought for the house—a strong bed that could handle vibrations, he said with a smile. He envied Mubarak, his sense of powerlessness intensified, and he felt that life was turning its back on him in a way he didn't understand. He set about painting the walls in Mubarak's house and whitewashing the ceiling, which was black from too much damp, cleaning the rooms and the courtyard, and in practice he became a servant at Mubarak's place in exchange for his board. Ashour the postmaster let him down again and Ousmane tried to blackmail him over the matter of the old man's pension but Ashour rebuked him, saying he was a portent of bad luck. He found himself drowning in misery. As for his ex-wife, apparently she hadn't been making empty threats: he was summoned to the police station after a complaint she had made against him. That happened after she sent him a sum of money with Oualid, their son. The money soon vanished and he came back asking for more. He was ravenously hungry and his dignity by then was a thing of the past. She rebuffed him on the second attempt but he persisted in hoping. I've recovered, try me, I'll work and bring you everything you ask for, he told her in a begging tone, but he was one aspect of a miserable life she had decided to renounce forever. She wouldn't go back to that hell again. She gave a loud laugh, then threatened him with prison if he came back, and she promised that with the children at the beginning of every month, she would send him enough money for him to live on. Money isn't everything, you cow, was his angry response to her, as if he really was turning down her suggestion. If he killed her it wouldn't solve any problem, though the revenge would gratify him. He had thought of doing it several times. And if you killed her elderly husband, she would inherit his money and come back to you a wealthy woman. That's what the devil whispered in his ear, but his fragility outweighed his hate for either of them. If you had any dignity you would have killed her in the first place, but now it's much too late, Mubarak told him. Ousmane was speechless, unable to make a single comment in response. He had sound reasons for seeking revenge. He thought of strangling her and pissing on her dead body in front of the damned old man, but he didn't have the courage to do that, he admitted to himself. He had become cowardly and weak. He could see her growing stronger day by day, while he was in permanent decline.

Hoda was anemic, and she assumed it was because she was tired and tense, but four days later she discovered that her guess was misplaced. She had a pregnancy test and it was positive. At the time she hadn't thought it possible. It seemed like the most unlikely thing that could happen to her. Rafik was impotent, at least that's what he thought. He was reluctant to talk to doctors and avoided telling her for fear of upsetting her or seeing pity for him in her eyes. So it was an ambiguous morning: her happiness was incomplete, tainted by the uncertainty, and the search for Rafik became more than justified, more than just a question of emotional games by which she intended to win his heart and live with him. He deserved it, now that he was the father to the child in her womb. She called him on the phone to give him the good news, but his phone was turned off. Then she headed to what was supposed to be their apartment, where their one and only orgasm had produced both a fetus and great uncertainty. She found the apartment empty, tidy, with some books lying on the sitting room table and a picture of him in his police uniform on the wall. A bedside lamp gave out a faint light and his clothes in the wardrobe were as they had been. The fridge was empty, except for a bottle of mineral water and some triangles of cheese. She wrote a small note asking him to contact her urgently and left it where he would easily notice it. She tried to call him dozens of times but to no avail. At night she felt guilty because she had kept away from him for longer than she should have. She speculated that he might have gone back to Mounira. First loves are never forgotten. She cursed him thoroughly, and then her thoughts wandered as far as thinking about going to see Mounira at her school to win him back from her. Mounira had had her chance with Rafik and had no right to begrudge Hoda her chance with him. Hoda had given him something that her rival had not been able to give him for ten whole years. She couldn't sleep and she wrestled with doubts all night long. The next day she went back to Rafik's place and he still wasn't there and she found the note she had written still in the same place. She knocked on the next-door neighbor's door. An old woman opened it and told her that since Rafik and his wife had separated she was no longer aware of his presence. Then Hoda had no other option but to ask after him in the police station where he worked.

She postponed that task till the next day, and during one of the longest waits she had ever endured, a thousand ideas occurred to her. He was mean and capricious and it would be best if she never found him. If he did come back he would torment her again every time. It would be best if she had an abortion and got that source of torment out of the way before disaster struck. She accused herself of being stupid—stupid in a way that very much pretended to be smart. Too many hasty judgments had landed her with an unborn child whose father she would never find. She loved him, and it made her happy that she was going to have a child with him, but she had little luck with men. This was another piece of evidence she could wave in the face of her mother, who claimed that her indifference was the reason. Now here she was, far from indifferent, looking for him, and she wanted him to be hers, if she could find him. She didn't want to lose hope. It was too soon to fall into despair, even if she felt it was pointless to reconsider the factors that she had discounted on her journey to the point that she had now reached.

When she went to see him, Police Commissioner Abdel Ouahab Chaal received her warmly. She was flustered and didn't know how to introduce herself to him and in what capacity she could ask after Rafik. Who was Hoda Ouanas to Rafik Nassiri? It was a short-lived but difficult test, and with his good judgment the commissioner shortened the task for her. Officer Rafik Nassiri is on a long leave of absence, he said in a dispassionate voice. Then he added in the same tone of voice: "Unfortunately I rarely speak to him on the phone. You know the pressures of work." She thanked him for his understanding and left his office. Half an hour later she decided to go for broke. She found herself parking her car outside the entrance to the Lycée Cheikh Bouamama where Mounira worked. She went in and found her. As they stood together, Hoda avoided looking her in the eye. She wasn't confident about what she was doing or whether this math teacher, Mounira Daoudi, deserved to be seen as her rival. Just as the governor had done, Mounira saved her from embarrassment and from making up an implausible lie. She didn't ask Hoda in what capacity she was asking about Rafik. She knew something about her, or maybe her female intuition came up with an expectation that was on the mark. The anxiety in Hoda's eyes gave everything away. They stood and faced each other with wary glances, in a silence charged with restrained hostility and a barrage of insults that they kept to themselves. They weren't capable of starting a battle to vent their ire when the prize had disappeared. "Has Rafik come back to you," Hoda asked Mounira, as if begging for a firm denial. "He disappeared I don't know how many days ago," Hoda added, lowering her tone to a sisterly voice that was excessively imploring and apologetic about her having won a heart that had been Mounira's. Mounira didn't say a word in reply, but after a few moments of silence, she shook her head. Finally they found something they could agree on—worrying about him. "I don't mind, I'm a married woman now." Mounira retained a striking severity when she told her that. She wanted to deny she was ready to agree with her on anything. She wasn't completely honest and she largely failed in concealing her interest. Hoda bowed her head in sorrow. She had hoped to learn from Mounira the places that Rafik frequented, but it didn't happen. She walked a few paces, then heard Mounira say, "Ask him to tell me he's okay, when he comes back."

Hoda called Commissioner Chaal and made an appointment to meet him. He had given her his phone number the last time. She had hesitated to call him but eventually she did. "Police work is very exhausting, it's slow-motion suicide if we were to describe it accurately," he said. "I'm sorry, I'm sorry, I've started grumbling a lot, you're always welcome and you can come the day after tomorrow, if Saturday would suit you," he added. She thanked him gratefully. "Not at all, I'm at your service, doctor." She thought of looking for a way to contact Rafik's family. He might be at his mother's. He had spoken about her once and he seemed very attached to her. He might have gone to her place to relax a little. But if he hadn't gone there? Then his mother would be anxious and he might be annoyed that she was being too intrusive. She kept thinking of some other way to ask after him. He had felt tired and gone back to his family to relax a little. That's what she hoped. He would come back, he had to come back. Friday passed ponderously and at nine o'clock on Saturday morning she was in the waiting room to go in and see the police commissioner. She had decided to submit a formal report on his disappearance. She was his wife and she had a right to be anxious about him.

The commissioner seemed understanding and he promised to make a special effort. Rafik was working under his command and he said he liked him. It wasn't hard for him to ask to check she was really his wife, with a proper marriage certificate. Rafik Nassiri had resigned from the department a while back, during the long leave of absence he had requested. "Okay, he was tired and I understood his desire," he said, telling her what he thought of Rafik leaving the police force before he was asked to leave. "I too would like to leave, doctor. We put up with everyone's delinquent behavior and we're expected to protect people from everyone's evil ways." He had heard the imam's sermon the day before, when the loudspeakers at the mosque were blaring out his powerful spiritual advice. He's an eloquent preacher, recently transferred from the Takoua mosque in the station district and appointed acting dean of the city's imams pending his confirmation in the post. He spoke about women who dress ostentatiously, the prevalence of adultery and fornication, and the practice of soliciting money from people under false religious pretenses. He nodded off a little during the sermon. Cheikh Hassan Daffaf was reciting in a stirring voice, while a torrent of thoughts was pushing him in every direction. The commissioner smoked two cigarettes while chatting to Hoda. He was tired and his jowls were drooping. He spoke to her about positions that Rafik had taken and said that the pressures on him because of that damned hotel business had taken a toll on him. He might be lying low until he calms down a little, he said. Her pride in Rafik grew, and she wanted to tell him that in her womb she was carrying someone who could bring Rafik back to life if Rafik heard of his existence, even if he was dead. The thoughts exhausted her. Rafik had retreated before winning. He could have won if he had waited a few more days, but he had admitted defeat prematurely. She submitted an official report on the disappearance of her husband, Rafik Nassiri. There was a short silence. She felt that the commissioner was losing interest as the minutes passed and, generally speaking, he was less interested in the case than she expected. She thanked him for nothing, then took her leave in the expectation that they would inform her of any new developments.

He escorted her to the lobby on the ground floor and stood there with her for some seconds. Then an aide interrupted him and he said goodbye and went back to his office, for them to tell him they had found the body of an old man in the cemetery. A young woman had died the previous day after a traffic accident and her family had gone to dig a grave for her, and then they found the old man's body. He had wire wrapped around his neck and his face had been disfigured with battery acid, probably so that he couldn't be identified. It wasn't suicide but a premeditated crime after a violent struggle, and his body showed clear signs of violence. The preliminary information showed that the victim was Mubarak Tahraoui, seventy-two years old, who owned a café in the station district and lived in a house nearby. He had five daughters, all of them married. In such cases the motive was probably money. A few days earlier Mubarak Tahraoui had gone away and he hadn't been back home, and yet his daughters hadn't submitted any report that he had disappeared. The cemetery custodian, Djelal Ben Hmida, known as Djelal Bleary Eyes, said he didn't know anything. He was in detention pending referral to the prosecutor's office. Abdel Ouahab Chaal heard all this from his aide without making any comment. Then he asked him about his man in the station district, Kada the Informer. Maybe he could tell us something, he said, disgruntled about everything. The aide replied that they had tried to contact him, without success so far. The policemen had been given instructions to remain on duty in the cemetery, which now had no custodian, until the department in charge of cemeteries in the capital managed to send someone to replace the caretaker. The commissioner went to the hospital and wanted to meet any members of the victim's family.

At the entrance to the emergency department, he met Hoda again and told her irritably that he couldn't sleep without sleeping pills. She had to come back to start her shift in the physiotherapy unit in half an hour, but curiosity had driven her to find out the reason for the commotion at the entrance. An ambulance had brought a dead body. It was a man in his fifties who had thrown himself in front of a train at about eight twenty in the morning. The passengers had been on the crowded platform waiting for the train to come to a complete halt so that they could get on. Ousmane La Gauche shut his eyes and threw himself onto the track. He had been seen a few minutes earlier smoking his last cigarette, sitting on a metal chair with his legs stretched out and without a care in the world, as if he were awaiting a routine appointment that didn't deserve any special attention.

Two days later she came back to meet the commissioner and ask him if they had made any progress on her husband, but he wasn't in his office, and the policeman at reception told her that he might not come that day. She left frustrated and, on her way to the hospital, she dropped in on a small post office. She decided to withdraw all her salary for that month and after that she asked for emergency leave so that she could spend all her time looking for him. Now that her pregnancy was confirmed, Rafik was worth more than just waiting around foolishly and fretting pointlessly over his disappearance. She made up her mind to fight her battle to the end and get Rafik back. All she hoped for was that he was well and nothing terrible had happened to him. She remembered that she had to buy a gift for Dalila Allak, a nurse who worked with her and who had invited her to her wedding. She thought she had a duty to stand by Dalila because she was unlucky. She reached the post office where she always went to withdraw the money she needed, and which was usually quiet. This time she found a team of inspectors inside checking the money, and the staff in a very tense state. The postmaster, who was called Ashour, was said to have disappeared the day before, leaving a large deficit in the cash balance. In the afternoon she got into her car with her colleagues who had also been invited to the wedding. She went unenthusiastically, to oblige the poor woman. She kept completely silent on the way to Bachdjer-rah, and at the party she seemed so worried that it was hard for her to do more than smile vacantly. After less than an hour she took her leave but the bride insisted she stay to see her new husband. She was in a white dress that was ridiculously tight on her plump body, and when her husband came in for them to be photographed together, the women made fun of her. Dalila Allak was happy with the slim bridegroom: she pulled him by the arm like a young girl who's been bought her first doll. Hoda was about to leave the party when Abdel Oua-hab Chaal called her and asked her to come immediately. She didn't notice the bridegroom coming in, but when she looked up and saw him, she knew it was much too late for anyone to do anything about it.

CPSIA information can be obtained
at www.ICGtesting.com
Printed in the USA
JSHW012140210922
30796JS00003B/5